THE

# URBANBOYS™
## DISCOVERY OF THE FIVE SENSES

"A wonderful and deeply written emotional adventure."
— *Self Publishing Review*

"An unforgettable and ultimately fulfilling rollercoaster ride that I won't soon forget!"
— *Sophia Diane, Indie Book Reviewers*

"Author K.N. Smith has at her disposal a lyrical prose that describes the environment and the characters in such fine (and magical) detail that you can't help but fall in love with the world she has created." — *Moterwriter Reviews*

"K.N. Smith has an incredible way with words. Her descriptions are vivid, you see what the characters are seeing, you feel what they are feeling. You feel like you are there." — *Cody Brighton, Indie Book Reviewers*

"*Discovery of the Five Senses* is easily the most originally crafted variation of young adult superhero themed books. Packed with crime-fighting action, drama, and plenty of the unexpected, this novel fills the pages with an enchanting story to remember." — *Cosmofixed, Goodreads*

"The author's matchless prose details cinematic fight sequences and fully developed characterizations especially in a final, stupendous scene that will take your breath away and leave you limp with spent emotions. Five stars for this imaginative and inspiring story, sure to be as appealing to general audiences as it will be to the YA crowd."
— *Don Sloan, Publishing Industry Reviewer*

"An emotional journey not soon forgotten, full of danger, conflict, tension, and drama!"
— *John Goldman, Book Reviewer*

K.N. Smith
Post Office Box 233553
Sacramento, CA 95823

Library of Congress Control Number: 2015913202

ISBN 9780989474757 (softcover)
ISBN 9780989474764 (e-book)
ISBN 9780989474788 (KDP)
ISBN 9780989474771 (audio book)

Manufactured in the USA

2nd Edition

*With brittle leaves and debris thrust upward, the two were enveloped in a dark, hazy hell as they engaged in a violent struggle for what seemed like an eternity.*

# Prologue

**A**N ALLURING MIDNIGHT seeped through the preserve, where huge, wavy leaves danced beneath the moonlight. The setting was suited for a late night encounter between two friends. But almost immediately, their conversation went awry.

"We've been here and there and everything's alright, I guess." Ross Dawson weighed his words. His eyes roamed away from his friend. "But you've changed. You're not the same."

An imposing Joaquin Grayson grabbed Ross's arm, squeezing it to the point of pain. "You don't think I'm capable of leading us in the right direction, do you? We can't stay here going nowhere. I chose you to go with me. We need to stick together!"

His long nails dug into Ross's skin, the piercing, half-moon impressions nearly bursting through. His flaming hand absorbed Ross's fear, the constricted flow of blood beating against his palm.

Ross bore the numbness of his arm. "Look at you. It's like I don't even know you anymore!"

"We've been doing fine for almost a year." A blush-wine color flooded Joaquin's cheeks. "Why do you want to cut out now?"

For the first time, Ross trusted himself to speak up, to question the mounting dissension clouding their friendship. "Man! Why do you need so much power?"

He remembered when a youthful adventure had first brought them to these forbidden woods. A place with tales of strange happenings, mysterious noises, and unsolved disappearances... or so it was said.

During that youthful adventure, they'd all changed. Then, *he'd* changed. And somehow, the misunderstood, glowing energy that had dripped from the huge leaves awakened a solo ambition fueled by wrought emotions.

Regardless, the two friends stood firm in the dark night.

Joaquin breathed deeply. As a result of Ross's questions, and while wondering what would happen to Ross's gift, he set his intention. He let go of Ross's arm and ran his fingers through his long, thick hair.

He stilled his lean, muscular frame, restraining the rising tension in his body, hiding any indication of his next move. Still clutching his hair, Joaquin closed his eyes, listening for Ross's movements. He knew he would not be able to turn back. *It's on me. I'm the only one who can build a new way of life.*

And in the absence of even a hint of an exchange, Joaquin spun around and lunged at Ross. He grabbed him by the throat, knocking him down.

With brittle leaves and debris thrust upward, the two were enveloped in a dark, hazy hell as they engaged in a violent struggle for what seemed like an eternity.

Ross flared up. "Get the hell off of me!"

Joaquin persisted. "What are you going to do, Ross? Where are you going to go?"

Ross scrambled to his feet, fighting back with a blow to Joaquin's head, followed by several body punches. Joaquin stumbled and fell, giving Ross those precious few seconds required for his escape.

Fueled by a rush of pulsating adrenaline, Ross ran frantically, stretching his quivering legs. His rich brown skin tightened as he pounded through the forest. He tried to ignore his thunderous heartbeat while scanning the pathways, searching for possible escape routes.

With his baseball cap lost to the wind, his short, curly hair had exposed to the open air. Ross grasped the moment, one littered with deep panic and a singular appreciation for survival.

This turn of events stemmed from countless episodes in which Joaquin, only nineteen yet extremely demanding, had tried to control those around him.

The violent exchange was the smoky glow at the end of a dark tunnel, and they had ventured across the breaking point inside this lush landscape.

ༀ

At the same moment, on the other side of the preserve, Della Sato and Juson Yamada examined the stars on this warm summer night. Although disturbing tales had contributed to the mystery of the forest for generations, it offered privacy unavailable in their everyday lives.

Juson stood beneath trees adorned with apple-green moss. "I know we're not supposed to be in here, but look at this place."

"I heard people got lost in here and they never came out," Della said, pulling back. "Do you think that's true?"

"No way," Juson convinced himself, unsure of the validity of the tale. "If someone gets hungry enough, they'll find their way out."

"Our neighbor said there were weird noises coming out of here one night," Della recalled, as she clutched her purse.

"That's not true. It looks safe in here." Juson took her by the hand. "Maybe their TV was up too loud. C'mon."

Della grasped Juson's bicep as she began to move her feet. Tiny lights greeted the couple. They set foot in the forest, walking and talking, looking for the perfect place to nestle. It was quiet, peaceful, and visually unlike what they had imagined.

❧

With his feet tearing across the forest floor, Ross's vision blurred, and he became lost in the darkness. Surrounded by a blackness offering no hope, layers of greenery swallowed him, slowing him down. But when the sharpness returned, a kaleidoscope of hues filled his eyes, and he tore through the brush.

Joaquin's labored breathing grew louder with each passing moment. He pressed his hands into the earth, feeling for the warmth of Ross's steps. He lifted his hands into the air, distinguishing wind patterns offering clues as to Ross's direction, validated by swaying leaves in the trees. Powerful nerve receptors in his fingertips quivered with the weight of his desires.

Forging ahead, he caught up with Ross.

He slammed Ross to the ground, wrapping his arm tightly around his neck. Joaquin's long hair whipped and swung, practically covering them both, stinging Ross's sensitive eyes.

Ross struggled against Joaquin's grip but was unable to break free. He finally managed to drive an elbow into Joaquin's ribs.

Joaquin gasped for air, loosening his hold long enough for Ross to wrench away and stagger to his feet. They exchanged a flurry of punches, jabs, and kicks, setting the bruising process in motion.

Despite fatigue setting in, Ross found the strength to circle behind Joaquin. He landed a ferocious blow to Joaquin's back, knocking him down yet again.

Catching his breath, Ross resumed his search for a way out of the preserve. His eyes cut across the landscape sharply.

But Joaquin took only moments to compose himself, his face returning to its expressionless state. His pursuit of Ross had resumed, and with furious determination.

❧

Beneath the glow of the moonlight, the appeal of the curvaceous foliage mesmerized Della and Juson.

Resting among fallen leaves deeper inside the preserve, Juson looked into Della's almond eyes and stroked her hair. "We'll be married someday. It's in the cards, you know. I really love you."

Della smiled softly. "I love you, too."

"You're smart, beautiful... creative." Juson caressed Della's slender waist. "I'm pretty sure all the guys are jealous of me right about now."

Della brushed Juson's face with her fingers. "Well, look who's talking... the handsome prince."

"We could make a nice home here and raise some kids." Juson tried to maintain a serious expression. "We'll have one to wash dishes and one to clean the house."

"Oh, really?" Della wrapped her leg around Juson. "Well, that means you'll be mowing the yard, mister."

His solid, athletic frame meshed with her delicate figure. Hidden behind a massive leaf, their passion spilled over. They drew in close and kissed with animated fervor, but the sickening sounds of a brawl interrupted.

"What the heck was that?" Juson whispered.

Trying to determine the direction of the commotion, he pressed his hand over Della's mouth. The look in his eyes signaled the need for silence. They peeked out briefly and saw the brutal fight.

Della began to shake. Shocked at the sight, she looked for an exit in the thick brush. Sensing she might dart away, Juson held her close.

As the fight continued, Joaquin landed multiple blows on Ross's head and took a few in return. He charged forward, pushing Ross into a tree where a low, protruding branch punctured his torso.

"Aargh!" Ross grasped the wound, screaming. His torn shirt absorbed the blood spilling out of the gash.

Branches cracked and fell around them, one whipping the leaf covering Della and Juson, but it quickly snapped back into place.

Ross stumbled over a branch and fell, landing just inches from Della and Juson, his body pressing against the leaf sheltering the two.

Fear silenced Della's panicked desire to cry out, as Juson protected her with his body.

Joaquin pounced on Ross, striking him in the face. He wrapped his hands tightly around Ross's neck, pressing his full weight into the evil act.

Ross's contorted face began to relax.

Saliva dripped from Joaquin's mouth as he squeezed tighter.

Ross's legs stopped twitching.

Joaquin waited for the end to arrive. The forest fell silent apart from his strained breathing.

It was over.

Joaquin collapsed beside the body.

Ross's empty, wide-open eyes expressed the sheer horror of his fate.

Exhausted, Joaquin stayed there for a few minutes while the forest absorbed the intentional, malicious act. Pained moans escaped him as he stood rubbing his eyes, which were suddenly burning.

Unable to see clearly, he stumbled out of the forest, going anywhere the night would take him. His eyes burned a furious, deep red. He would remain in an agonized condition for three long days.

Terrified, Della and Juson guessed at what had just happened. Afraid to move, they had no choice but to show more patience than they had thought possible in their lifetimes. The scared couple clung to each other, wondering what new horror awaited them.

The minutes seemed like hours, but they remained still, even as a bright light swept through the preserve. The light was sharp, electric against the blanket of darkness. It brought with it a clicking noise, which drove its way into their ears with a musical rhythm.

As the light zoomed in closer to Ross, it pounced against the leaf covering the two, then went dark as the clicks faded.

As the night progressed, Della and Juson found the courage to make their move. In disbelief, they ran home, holding a frightening secret in their hearts. A secret of murder, committed under a striking, glowing moonlight on the most fateful night of their young lives.

Mrs. Perkins knew a lot about the history of Danville Heights. But it was clear to her—some secrets were not to be revealed. The trick? Imitating the blades' mastery of secrecy throughout the decades.

# One

## *Twenty Years Later*

THE COMMUNITY OF DANVILLE HEIGHTS offers the scenic route to a carefully crafted universe. Casts of shadows cool and soothe, beckoning the weary, comforting their plight. Explosions of color captivate, blanketing the land. A peaceful valley filled with families disinterested in city life, its combination of natural resources and quaint charm enchant those fortunate enough to dwell within.

Nature expressed itself always, as seen in a swirling butterfly as it dipped toward a crimson landing pad. It meandered along clean streets where comfortable homes with large porches seemed to have been plucked from the pages of a country interiors magazine.

Sunlight showered a dwelling with pale mint and creamy white paint, warming the sun porch and a shallow saucer of water left for visiting birds.

The butterfly swooped to examine embellished mailboxes, flapping its orange wings as though it were clapping for the winner. One of the mailboxes read: Parker Residence.

A bike lay sideways in the yard.

In this town, folks enjoy ripe tomatoes, fragrant peaches, and loads of neighborly warmth. People were glad to see each other, or at least they understood the politeness of saying hello. After all, a warm smile that's always on the menu is reassuring indeed.

༞

Across the way, the morning sun seeped into the bedroom of Kinsu Yamada, an athletic teenager named after an uncle from Japan. *I'm so tired. It's time to get up, but I'd rather be dreaming about what's her name from sixth period. The girl with the short hair. Dang, what is her name anyway?*

Getting up now offered a downside, like chancing a nap in the middle of class. Because his sore muscles needed a stretch, the option of dreaming quickly disappeared, so he reached for the headphones on his nightstand.

"Let's see, how did that beat go?" He sifted through rhythms floating in his mind, like the masterpiece he had laid down yesterday. *One, two, dat, boom. Yeah, that's it right there! Only the beat master could do that.*

He pushed the blankets aside, then reached across his bed. *Where's my tablet?* He felt around until his fingers slid across cool metal. "In you go, headphones." He fired up one of his own tracks. The pulse of the beat brought him to life, but it wasn't complete. New sounds were destined to mingle with the melody. *I love this software.* "Alright, FastBeats, let's go."

Kinsu opened the dashboard. Black and white keys made interesting noises. He wove drum and guitar effects into his tracks, dragging and dropping them into perfect position. *Ooh, nice!*

With the track finished, a quick scroll through a beat-making contest announcement boosted his confidence. *I'm sure I can win this one. When is it? A few weeks from now? No problem. I got this!*

Time was moving. He plugged the headphones into his phone. A shuffled playlist spilled into his ears.

Kinsu rolled out of bed to look outside. The beat throbbed in his head. A bird flew by the window as the blinds sliced through the view of a picture-perfect morning in Danville Heights.

༄

A solid rocking chair made of real wood stood in the corner of the porch. It had beautiful grain and curves, just the way Mrs. Perkins remembered from her childhood. At seventy-five, she rocked almost daily, usually late at night, and like today, early in the morning before the sun peeked through sprawling trees.

She moved across her porch to adjust the hanging pots lined with moss, swaying in the soft wind. "Don't you look lovely?" Mrs. Perkins stroked the dark purple geraniums, gifted to her by an acquaintance. "Such a rare color. So beautiful."

She reached up to untangle a stubborn chain on one of the pots, which had caused it to lean sideways. *Much better,* she thought, after a few yanks.

A quiet town near the small city of Sandry Lake, Danville Heights was just the kind of place she liked. Small community feel. Occasions to get to know residents. Moments to find out their business. Just the way she liked it.

As she admired her flowers, something special met the morning. When the sun had appeared, sparkling dew evaporated from tall blades of grass, retracting the moisture so refreshing to the blades. Drying out right before her eyes, each blade had a story to tell emerging into the new day. So many stories. Much like the ones Mrs. Perkins had in memory.

She knew a lot about the history of Danville Heights. But it was clear to her—some secrets were not to be revealed. The trick? Imitating the blades' mastery of secrecy throughout the decades.

She gripped the arms of the rocking chair, lowering herself, landing on a striped pillow. *So comfortable. So nice and quiet.*

She looked to the sky and smiled.

The motion of the rocking chair was part of the puzzle of the day's awakening. Boys were slowly rolling out of bed, and the coffee was on, the rich aroma wafting through the houses. All of it made for a smooth transition from night to day without interruption of normal events.

∾

A few streets over, Chase Freeman, a junior at Danville Heights High School, had fallen in love with his pillow. But he could hear Diane, his older sister, moving around the house. She had been raising him since their single mother passed away two years ago from breast cancer. They were doing their best to make it from semester to semester.

Diane was definitely in charge. She kept the house in order doing what her mother would have done. "Lasagna tonight, loaded baked potatoes tomorr—" She saw her reflection in the computer monitor as she zoomed around a corner. "Let me check my grades on the portal."

She removed a small laundry basket from beneath her arm, setting it on the floor. With her knee on the desk chair, she logged-in to her online college courses to review the rankings. "B+? I was hoping for an A." She searched for the message icon and tapped the keys. *Dear Professor, I'd like to discuss this assignment during office hours...*

As Chase entered his junior year, she gave her all to keep him focused. A challenging job for a young woman, but it appeared to be working so far.

Chase loved to sleep, but it wasn't meant to be this morning. If he was going to catch a ride with Diane, he had to get up... now.

With her grades reviewed, she was on the move.

Diane passed his room while putting away the laundry. "Chase, you must not want a ride today." She could sense his fancy for feet dragging.

Chase jumped to the floor, suspending his covers in one hand. "Okay, okay, I'm up, see?" Tossing the blankets aside, he grabbed a silver bat from the corner of his room. *Step up to the plate.* He perfected his swing in the mirror. *Nothing can stop this player. One more season after this year, then I'll be an outfielder in college.*

Diane was still in the hallway. "No, I don't *see* anything. Get moving. I have to work at the café this morning."

Chase swung one more time. "I *am* up."

He bid farewell to his warm sanctuary. His deep brown skin glistened in the sunlight. A banner above the door with a quote from Babe Ruth caught his eye—'Every strike brings me closer to the next home run.'

Often amused with her brother, Diane smiled as she gave her final warning, "You'd better be, or you're walking, mister."

&#x221E;

There was no sign of the sun in the not so distant town of Sandry Lake. Considering the height of the east side buildings which should have received a golden kiss by now, this seemed odd.

Didn't the rooftops feel lonely awaiting the moment to greet the sun's fresh rays?

Usually, there was plenty of action on the road, but today the mood was low. A dark contrast to the bonds being made in Danville Heights, where the sun appeared to believe it had a multitude of friends on which to rely for the next stretch of time.

*His eyes revealed a sliver of perceived childhood trauma. Feeling lonely and unloved, second and not first. Feeling left out. Internal anguish spilled over, and his eyes lost all motion.*

# Two

## *Angry Tears*

A BLANKET OF DEEP CHARCOAL moved about like a sprawling, smoggy mass high above Sandry Lake, bringing gloom for all to see. The town was not as far from Danville Heights as one would guess. The approximate three-mile span between the two towns was actually close.

Compact houses and tenements sat near generous open spaces not far from the river. Simply designed storefronts personified the town—a no-frills place to live—suitable for those shunning a beaten path.

Sandry Lake had as few citizens as when it was first established. Most of its residents had escaped in the name of self-preservation, deserting their comfortable dwellings. Elected officials had run away, fearing the evil that had swarmed in.

Coming up from beneath the shadows in unexpected moments of terror, someone had assumed control of the town, twisting the meaning of what it was to be a community. The speed at which it had happened over the past few weeks had stunned the residents.

Clean streets had filled with trash. Broken glass littered the landscape. Doors had been kicked in. And a blackness, like a blanket of hell, begged to be lifted.

There were two factions at hand: the last of the committed citizens hanging on to the end, and a cruel, malicious force.

A gang of hooligans roamed Sandry Lake at all hours, stealing from citizens, beating them up at will. The town's small, volunteer security force, which had been surrounded and overwhelmed, was unable to alert the neighboring police department.

The residents' hearts were filled with memories of when Sandry Lake had been a model community. They had used their own hands to build the town. To have what was rightfully theirs stolen was an atrocity none could fathom.

Although the faithful inhabitants had not given up, their manpower had waned. Their counterattack had become a waiting game, and they struggled to survive.

෨

The goons referred to him as *he*, likely not even knowing his name. With their washed minds, most had forgotten their own names.

After terrorizing numerous towns, *he* was focused on getting back home to... Danville Heights.

Closer than ever before, Sandry Lake merely served as a pit-stop for his selfish ways.

*He*... was Druth.

Like a fallen angel, he had turned evil, staging crimes to run folks out so he could command the scene.

"Hold it right there. Slow and steady." Druth eyed the lock on a steel door. "Hang on... wait for my word."

His chief henchman, Omar, complied. "Got it, boss."

"Now listen, here's how you take over a town. First you cut the power, then the cell towers. Shut down those fake security-bots. Robots, guards, whatever you call them. Bot-cops are no threat. You hear me?"

Omar sucked up to Druth. "Yeah, that's right. Then take their food supply and it's all good, boss."

"The most important part? A takeover map. Draw it out. I don't care if you use crayons, we need a lay of the land, and I mean the entire area including the surrounding towns."

"Yeah, I remembered, boss. We already started on the map."

"Alright, I'll take a look. Hang on... hold steady."

"We got the roads blocked, too, boss."

"Shut up! I said hold steady. Okay, wait... now!"

Druth swung the hammer.

*Bang!*

The lock went flying.

"Search this building. Bring any supplies you guys find." Druth talked tough in front of his gang. "And if you find any food, don't eat it all!"

"We hear you, boss." Omar evil-eyed nearby thugs. "Don't we, guys?"

"I'll be back." Druth made a fast exit.

He had been surviving in the depths for quite some time. Not understanding his own emotional insecurities, Druth had somehow become comfortable with madness, which was now in the director's chair of Sandry Lake. His brand of chaos had led him to the loneliest of places. And there, he reveled freely.

Druth walked aimlessly. The dark night deepened, drawing him in. *The favorite one. It was supposed to be me.* Angry tears surfaced. *I'm almost there. Soon, I'll be all-powerful and perfect… for my parents.*

Distorted thoughts had never escaped him.

Lost years, age chasing his parents. Time was of the essence. Homebound, his acute senses drove his twisted will.

And from where did this emerge?

His eyes revealed a sliver of perceived childhood trauma. Feeling lonely and unloved, second and not first. Feeling left out. Internal anguish spilled over and his eyes lost all motion.

Actual or imagined, his hurt was real. But it would not slow him down on his journey to destruction.

❧

"Grab those boxes over there and take them to our place," Omar said. "And don't drop anything! All we need is banged up food."

Four thugs nodded like puppets.

"I'm heading to the dock. I'll meet you there. Hurry up!" Omar yelled, a box tucked under his arm. He stepped over strewn trash on the empty streets of Sandry Lake. As he walked, he heard something unusual, like sniffing, whimpering. Omar saw Druth's shadow. "Boss, is that you? Is everything okay over there?"

"Keep moving, Omar. I'm good." Druth ducked behind a building, wiping his tears. "Stay on the guys."

Omar shrugged it off. "Alright, I'm on it."

A light wind swept through the air.

As Omar turned around, a firefly-looking light ball whizzed across his face. *Jeez... what the hell was that?*

He stepped back, dropping his package, something he told the thugs not to do.

Druth's voice lacked amusement. "Man, I swear... you don't listen. I said keep moving!"

Bending down to pick up the box, Omar observed the swirling pattern of the light ball circling through Sandry Lake. Darting in and out of buildings and trees, it turned around, advancing toward him.

"Get out of here!" His arms swept about wildly. He could see the little being racing to the sky.

It flew away, heading straight toward Danville Heights, taking with it news of the arrival of Druth and his rowdy gang of crusty hooligans.

*The succulent, their life-source of which they were fiercely protective, was the lushest of all the greenery in the preserve, and it beckoned.*

# Three
## *The Naculeans*

**F**LOATING WITHIN A BACKSTORY somewhere inside a swirl of time, soft balls of light had landed in the preserve, and from there, they had grown. Originating from the land of Naculea, the beings were pleasant. As promoters of peace, they had chosen the forest for its tranquil environment and natural amenities.

Collecting nectar from a single plant was also a life-giving reason for their journey. The succulent, their life-source of which they were fiercely protective, was the lushest of all the greenery in the preserve, and it beckoned.

The nectar gave the Naculeans energy. It allowed them to live. It caused them to glow. The liquid was a source of empowerment, for them, and others.

The beings had relaxed, knowing their best allies—the peaceful humans of Danville Heights—were nearby. After all, wouldn't their life-source be safe in a tranquil valley?

Perhaps, but cooperation from the humans would be needed to silence any real threats to ensure the survival of the species—a complex, double-edged sword, indeed.

As what looked like a round firefly swirled in from above, an exchange occurred between two thirsty light beings glowing with circular layers. Their language, which sounded like clicking noises, rang out in the preserve.

The first being floated among large fronds. "It is chosen."

"We must endure," the second one said.

"We must have the nectar. It is special. A gift to the world. There is no other way. We must protect the nectar and the people."

Rings of light, glowing deeper, richer toward the center like a bullseye, defined their weightless bodies. Feathered edges billowed against the darkness.

"Apart from Naculea, this is our home. We must find a way to divide the plant, to propagate, and grow more of the source to survive."

"It is the chosen way. The nectar is life. It brought peace here many years ago, but the help we sought eluded us."

"We must persevere for our survival, and to protect the people. But danger is near."

"Druth, the one who strayed, must be stopped. He is near, yet far from the intention of the gift."

Soft swirls of light rose, dissipating as they spoke.

"The others are capable, but they need our help. Peace will not come easily. We must give them strength."

"Druth will destroy our home. He will hurt the gifted ones if the nectar finds him."

"They will not survive him."

"The others must seek the will for survival. They must understand their own power."

A transient suspension held the beings in the preserve. Faint flecks of light dotted the landscape.

"In these two worlds, our ideas converge, yet collide."

"He must be stopped!"

"It is true."

"Naculea must endure."

"It is chosen."

Now resting upon the succulent, running rich with the life-giving nectar, the beings absorbed its energy, glowing as bright as the sun.

Thirst became a distant need yet again.

"We must warn... the one."

"The one who sees."

"The one who sees and hears much."

"It is the only way."

Final clicks faded into silence.

The little firefly-looking light ball whipped through the leaves. As though it had received a command, it spiraled toward the dark sky on a mission... to warn the one who sees and hears much.

*Russell was often in deep thought about Talia's downward spiral and its fatal conclusion. His blank stare mirrored the look on her face as her hand had pulled the wheel across the center divide, into the path of another car.*

# Four
## *Unevenly-Aged Twins*

"**L**EXICOGRAPHY—the work of writing a dictionary. Proscenium—an arch framing for a conventional stage. Erythrocyte? So... why do I need to know that word?" Mason Parker begrudged, flipping through the dictionary which had practically become one of his best friends. "Mature red blood cells containing hemoglobin. We need to know the spelling and definition. Okay, I get it."

Students in his sixth-grade class scoring at least eighty-five percent on tomorrow's super-sized test would receive a certificate for a free burger from the café where Diane worked.

*I'm getting that hamburger*, he thought, as he reviewed the second assignment: a short essay. "What do I want to be when I grow up? A newspaper reporter, of course. Wait, or maybe an author, or I might write short stories." His journalistic path to wonder and discovery had yet to be defined. "Maybe all of them."

Mason and his older brother, Jordan Parker, looked like unevenly-aged twins with big waves in their hair.

Their striking eyes gave pause to those meeting them for the first time.

"A newspaper reporter. Maybe that's what my essay could be about. Let's see… what stories would I write?" Mason's index finger rose to his lips, which were smashed together, twitching. *The Billiards Park grand opening? It's pretty quiet here, so there's not much excitement. Fishing in the river? Naw. What about falling into the river while fishing? Now, that's a story!*

He made a few notes, then yelled downstairs, "Hey, Dad, is breakfast ready?"

Their father, Russell Parker, had substantial dimples that handsomely framed his thick mustache. The small waves in his salted hair looked distinguished, as did his warm grin.

The boys' mother, Talia Platero, a gifted television producer, was a curvaceous beauty who had captured Russell's heart during their two-year courtship. They had married, but things derailed when the swish of a bottle entered the picture as an unwelcome guest in an otherwise unblemished scenario.

Russell was often in deep thought about Talia's downward spiral and its fatal conclusion. His blank stare mirrored the look on her face as her hand had pulled the wheel across the center divide, into the path of another car. *Darn those two-lane roads with nothing in between but hope and a prayer.*

"In a minute," Russell replied, as he kissed Talia's high school yearbook photo, returning it to the shelf.

Wrinkles set into Mason's forehead. "Dang, a whole minute? I'm hungry." With no choice but to wait for his meal, he dug deeper to find the next word. "Exfoliate—to scrub skin with a gritty substance to remove the dead surface layer." With his highlighter, he marked the word with a squeaky orange circle.

With his schoolwork organized, Mason bounced to the kitchen to get some pancakes. He sat, gripping a fork with great anticipation, staring curiously at the batter's bubbles in the hot pan.

Jordan strolled in and opened the refrigerator to find a carton of milk.

"Hey!" Mason shouted, jumping to his feet.

"It's mine, little man." Jordan wrapped his lips around the container's opening, chugging away.

"I know you hate that, Mason," Russell explained, sensing tension around the potential of backwash in the milk—a furious pet peeve of Mason's. "So, I bought him his own carton."

Jordan paraded the carton in the air. "Yeah, Dad bought me my own milk, so I'll drink as much as I want. Okay?"

Mason shrugged, mumbling, "Whatever."

Jordan wiped his mouth with his shoulder, the liquid absorbing into his shirt.

Mason reached for the comics, searching for the strip with the big, red dog. "Dad, can a dog actually be that big? Bigger than people? Where do you get that kind of dog?"

Russell had already accepted the fact that one of the side effects of a gifted student is they ask a ton of questions. Mason had always been curious about the *whys* of life. His dad and brother did the best they could to satisfy his thought-provoked mind.

Russell looked to Jordan for an endorsement of his buried laugh. "It's just a cartoon, Mason."

As Jordan secretly acknowledged his dad, his cell phone rang. It was Ronald Berry, a tough wide receiver from the football team.

Jordan swiped the screen. "Hey, what's up?... Today?... What?... Are you serious?... After yesterday's practice, I don't know if I can handle more drills!"

Coach Thomas wanted extra conditioning before the big game against Markley High School on Saturday night. Jordan was in Ronald's team phone tree. It was Ronald's job to deliver the bad news. But to an overworked, sore player, this was the worst news, especially in the middle of pancakes with crispy edges.

Jordan's eyes rolled to the back of his head. "Okay, dude, see you at school."

Russell peeked over the newspaper. "Sounds like you'll be home late again."

"I'd rather be out late with a girl," Jordan mumbled, staring at his cold, syrup-soaked pancakes.

Russell savored the last of his coffee. "What?"

"I mean, yes," Jordan respectfully clarified. "The game against Markley is going to be a battle, but we're up for it."

"No worries, you guys got this. Mason and I will be there to show some love." Russell searched for his car keys. He needed to hear a jingle or else he'd be late for work. He found the keys next to the bread basket. "Alright guys, I'll see you later."

"Bye, Dad," the boys said.

Jordan rubbed his arms and neck. His fist met the counter with a double thud. "Five minutes, Bud."

"Sir, yes sir!" Mason stood, saluting in the middle of the kitchen. "Packed and ready to go, sir!"

*Jordan didn't see anything, but he had heard something, like a multitude of noises getting louder, coming out of nowhere.*

# Five
## *Predestination*

**W**ITH FIVE MINUTES TO GO, Mason cleared the plates and wiped the table. He stuffed cups into the dishwasher which had barely closed when a shattering thud hit the front door.

*Bam!*

With its fury, it almost broke the glass.

Mason spun around, facing the door. "What the—" He cracked the curtain open, taking a quick peek at the commotion outside.

Kinsu stretched his arms. "Markley on Saturday night and you're *catching* like that?" His palms met the sky.

"Markley on Saturday night and you're *throwing* like that?" The football team's right guard, Rhee Smith, defended himself. "That was all on you, bro. Are you sure you're ready?"

Playfully, they punched each other.

Rhee grabbed the football. His build paired nicely with his dark blue jeans and white T-shirt.

Mason opened the door slowly.

"Hey, sorry about that." Rhee sensed Mason's discomfort with the rude intrusion. "Are you ready to go? Where's Jordan?"

Mason folded his arms into a pretzel. "He's coming."

Jordan rushed downstairs. "Come on, Bud." He grabbed the last of his stuff. "Let's bounce."

In a show of brotherhood, Kinsu punched Jordan on the shoulder as he came down the steps.

Jordan rubbed his sore muscles. "Good morning to you, too, Kinsu."

"Sorry, dude, but I'm all pumped up." Kinsu's fists went flying through the air. "I entered a beat-making contest. I'm sure I can win. The grand prize is a two-thousand-dollar college scholarship, and the winning beat gets featured on a TV commercial."

"Really?" Jordan said. "Cool!"

"Yeah, there's a series of challenges, then I have to upload the finished track in a few weeks."

Jordan reassured Kinsu. "You got this, man."

Rhee grabbed Mason. "See, that's why we're friends, because we can act any way we want and say anything to each other." He rubbed his knuckles into Mason's head. "We've got each other's backs."

Mason tried to wriggle away. "Yeah, I know."

"Aren't you glad you have so many big brothers watching out for you?"

"I guess I am," Mason said. *Now, can you please get your stupid knuckles off my head?*

༄

Druth took to the streets of Sandry Lake in dark jeans, dark shoes, and a dark jacket. His clothes mirrored his mood, the rips and tears emulating his emotions.

He peered into a storefront where social gatherings had once taken place, seeing spilled coffee beans, overturned chairs, and neon signs, lifeless, like the dead. He turned to see one building after the other, dilapidated, all gasping for air.

Electricity had been cut off, igniting the shutdown, limiting the residents' abilities to see their way to safety. The storefronts, too, ached for light.

He walked to the adjacent building—an office hub. *Pens. Markers. Paper.* His raised boot met the glass door, shattering it.

Reaching through to unlock the knob, he stepped over the crunchy mess to find office supplies. *Can't finish the map without these.* He grabbed a pack of markers and mechanical pencils.

Druth found his way to the edge of town, noting streets and structures, all cast with a grayish tint, reflecting the solemnness of the situation.

He reached into his pocket and pulled out the map drawn by Omar and the goons. *What is this?* Kindergarten scribbles. Squares and stick figures. Squiggly lines. *I swear...*

He sat on the hard earth, smoothing out some fresh paper. Gliding a black marker, he quickly produced a detailed scene encompassing three towns: Danville Heights, Sandry Lake, and Lavender Quarry, bordering the Stanton Bridge.

*I need to see all of it at a glance, all together. Roads, stores, houses, police stations, banks... all of it.* Fine details dotted the page, with room for more to come.

Pickets splashed across the paper, adjacent to billowy trees, eleven blocks in on the Danville Heights sketch. A home stood marked with an X. *Mom, Dad.* A tear fell from his cheek, smashing into the paper, swelling the ink on the page.

He became overwhelmed with a desire to gaze upon his parents' home. Still battling hurtful thoughts, Druth set out for Danville Heights.

೨

The boys got on with their walk. Their first stop was Mason's school, Cane Rapids Elementary School, just down the street from Danville Heights High School.

"Hey, Bud. Don't forget my late practice." Jordan switched his books to his other arm. "You can walk home with your friends, okay?"

"Alright, but when will you be home?" Mason asked.

"Probably after Dad, so remember to lock up."

Perfect temperature, a staple of the land, graced the friends. Sweet chirps floated through the air, gifting greetings to all.

Skies were spattered with two kinds of blue: a deep quenching hue far along the color palette, and a softer shade suited for an innocent cherub. A subject for endless gazing, these complexions stood together to create a canvas for the outstretched oaks.

The branches reached for one another like half-curved interlocking fingers. Standing beneath the sparse awning, the boys kept walking, never looking upward.

The light ball, sitting atop one of the oak branches, observed. It puffed up, charting a course straight toward Jordan and Kinsu, who were walking behind Rhee and Mason.

Stealthy and steady, it meandered through the air as if it were on a trapeze. When it reached Jordan and Kinsu, it exhaled without making a sound, softly sprinkling its dust above their heads.

Jordan and Kinsu inhaled microscopic particles, not even causing a sneeze. Traveling through their mouths and nostrils, bits of energy made their way across mucus and bone, being absorbed instantly.

The light ball continued gliding, curving upward and out of sight.

Jordan swiped at his ear.

A bit of fluid appeared in Kinsu's eyes. He dabbed them on his shoulders, wicking the moisture away.

With only minutes before school, everyone picked up the pace, but Jordan slowed down.

Rhee turned around and took notice of Jordan's peculiar expression. "What's up, dude?"

Jordan turned his head sideways. "I hear a loud swarm of birds. Do you hear that?" He pulled his ear to make his hearing more accurate, standing half crouched, ready to duck below the fowl.

"Do I hear what?" Rhee scanned the area. "What does it sound like?"

Jordan was sure he heard something, which caused pain in his ears. It was now higher pitched. "You guys don't hear anything?" His eyes tightened as he pushed against his ear.

The group examined Jordan. As if on an island by himself, he struggled with the achy echoes floating in and out of his ears.

ॐ

Druth arrived in Danville Heights, moving about briskly, hiding behind shrubbery and cars. His hands met surfaces, from fences to foliage, to get a feel for the environment. He dragged his nails softly along the tree trunks.

*Fifteen homes on this street. And the bakery... just where it used to be.* He scribbled notes and drew sketches on his Danville Heights rendering. *This town looks the same, so this won't be hard.*

He crept along, peeking through bushes. He saw the boys, and watched them from a distance.

When he saw Jordan and Mason, his emotions welled. Their eyes were identical to someone he had known long ago. *It can't be!*

Like large almonds, captivating in their shape and color, Jordan and Mason's eyes beautifully expressed their mixed heritage, showcasing a mash of brown, green, and blue. Reminiscent of a seascape, their dark eyelids and thick eyebrows perfectly framed their blue-hazel features.

Peeping from high above in the trees, the fluttering light ball saw Druth watching the boys. It spun around and bounced upon a branch, rattling the leaves.

Druth looked up to see what it was. The light ball's translucent frame quickly extinguished its energy source. It became see-through and hid from Druth.

Jordan bent down and shook his head. His hearing finally returned to normal.

Mason looked worried. "Are you okay?" He touched his brother's arm.

"Yeah, I'm okay," Jordan assured Mason, stroking the waves in his little brother's hair.

Rhee kept one eye planted on Jordan. "Are you sure you don't have water in your ears, aqua boy?"

The guys pushed Jordan, who mustered half a smile. "Water... maybe?" He glanced around in what seemed like slow motion. He'd been swimming plenty of times and knew what water in his ears felt like, and this was not that.

Jordan didn't see anything, but he had heard something, like a multitude of noises getting louder, coming out of nowhere. But time was ticking. "Let's move. I hate begging for late slips."

As they walked, Druth was struck by the thought of his discovery, but his mission kept him moving toward his parents' home. He stuffed the map into his pocket and walked in another direction.

The light ball flew to the sky. It passed Mrs. Perkins, who was rocking on her porch. Hovering for a moment, it sped away to alert the Naculeans about Druth.

Mason took out his notes, rattling off yet another word on the super-sized test. "Predestination. A predetermined destiny."

His eyes, weighted with concern, met Jordan's as they pushed forward on the final stretch toward school.

*The simple, manicured residence began hacking its way through Druth's emotions. Tiny taps, huge whacks, tearing across memories pleasant and painful.*

# Six

## *Left Out*

**L**IKE AN AIR COURIER shepherding precious cargo on a strict deadline, Jordan kept a protective hand on Mason. Getting him to school safely and on time was his job. His father made it clear this was what he expected, warning Jordan to never fail his family.

Jordan walked Mason into the school-yard. "Alright, little bro, have a good day." He wrapped his arm around Mason's shoulder.

Mason gripped Jordan's waist. "Are you sure you're okay?" He knew Jordan was not joking about having heard something. Although he seemed back to normal, he was concerned about his big brother.

"I'm fine, don't worry," Jordan said.

Mason walked into the school-yard, met some friends, and was off to start his day.

As Jordan, Rhee, and Kinsu walked toward Danville Heights High School, the beauty of the scenery magnified, framing them like subjects tangled in a luscious piece of art.

Lush foliage coursed the scene. Complement pops of colorful, fall flowers brought a touch of joy to their morning route. In the distance, the soothing voice of the river brought calm to the surrounding greenery.

At school, two girls waved at Jordan. After all, he was a popular running back on the football team. His impressive physique sure attracted the ladies.

"You take one, I'll take the other," Rhee insisted, slicking his golden hair.

Jordan made a beeline for the girls. "Keep dreaming. I've got this covered all by myself." Hugging both of them, he darted to class.

Rhee shook his head. "Jerk."

As Rhee and Kinsu entered the campus, a girl walked toward them. She stood out like a sea of lusciousness waiting to be discovered by a lonely explorer.

Kinsu's eye shifted to her skirt, flowing in the wind. "She likes me."

Rhee was looking just as hard as Kinsu.

Although his tongue was twisted in knots, Kinsu kept moving in the direction of the crowd. "Man, she's fine."

He waved at her, trying to be cool.

Rhee pointed toward the classroom. "C'mon, dude, the bell's about to ring."

Everyone made it inside before the bell except for Kinsu. He finally turned to enter the room, meeting the door frame with a harsh reality.

*Whack!*

He took it in stride as the students laughed at his infectious goof appeal, and what must have been a sore forehead.

৯৯

Sunlight spilled through the leaves, projecting an abstract pattern on the lawn. A home's brick exterior had held its appeal for decades, the embellished mailbox not quite to its glory, but still colorful.

The simple, manicured residence began hacking its way through Druth's emotions. Tiny taps, huge whacks, tearing across memories pleasant and painful. Like a well cradled deep below the Earth's surface, Druth's eyes filled with fluid with the tightening of his jaw.

*I'll keep my distance for now, but I'm coming back.* A promise made to his parents, sitting on the other side of the brick and plaster, separated by boards, wires, and caverns of pain. The lack of connection ate into his soul. *I just need to complete my mission, to show them how powerful I can be.*

He turned to leave, noticing a blue bin on the side of the house where his childhood toys had once been stored.

He thought back to his ninth birthday. His trucks and toys had been too voluminous for his closet. *Dad stuffed everything in that blue bin.*

And while the birthday presents were pleasing, it had been days after the party before he would see them.

Dark in his childhood moods, he would often rest after emotional episodes.

*I was 'resting' when I turned nine. Those kids devoured my cake anyway. My own sibling waved a candle in my face. The decorations were for me. The cake was for me, not them. I'll have my day. I just need the gifts.*

Druth moved closer to the home. *I wonder if those toys are still in there.* But an approaching vehicle interrupted his moves. He slid behind a tree to wait it out.

A childhood melody traveled through his mind, tugging at him. He recalled the flicker of the candle near his eye. Quiet streets signaled him to push forward. He began walking but stayed out of sight, choking on bitter thoughts in his estranged hometown.

*Kinsu's eyes stretched way beyond the school, staring long and hard, focusing on what looked like rapid motion or some type of fluttery movement in the distance.*

# Seven
## *Beyond the Window*

WITH PREDICTABLE TIMING, the bell rang. As if the Kinsu show weren't enough, another student, Alex Morales, ran into the classroom. Crashing into his seat, he tipped toward the floor while looking at his girlfriend, Josie Perez, who was choking back a silent chuckle.

Alex was close to the other boys. As a group, they had discovered wondrous things over the years, and had often relied on him to un-jam them in sticky situations.

Mr. Knowlton, a tall, slender science teacher with a dense, cowboy-era mustache and thick-rimmed glasses, entered the room.

He put a formula and problem on the board. "Figure it out, people, and no talking or lookie-looing, either." He examined the tardy Alex. "Keep your eyes to the paper... and good luck."

Mr. Knowlton's choppy hair darted in all directions, inciting laughter from the students, but in a hushed manner for fear of an automatic *F* on a problem they had yet to solve. As would be expected of the unprepared, paper shuffling and pencil twirling ensued.

Four minutes later, Kinsu put down his pencil. His eyes traveled around the room to a bookshelf... then to a poster describing DNA... and lastly, out the window.

His eyes stretched way beyond the school, staring long and hard, focusing on what looked like rapid motion or some type of fluttery movement in the distance.

He saw a streak of light cross the sky. *Whoa!*

Color painted his view with wisps of undiscovered hues.

Mr. Knowlton approached Kinsu, interrupting his concentration. "Done already? Turn your paper over, Kinsu."

After doing so, Kinsu went back to staring out the window. *Is someone running on the road?*

Rhee watched Kinsu, wondering what had caught his eye. *What's he looking at?*

"Time's up, people," Mr. Knowlton announced. Loud moans filled the room. "Did anyone figure out the problem?"

Three students gave wrong answers.

Mr. Knowlton turned to Kinsu. "Is there an answer?"

Kinsu fought to break his fixation.

"Hello... Earth to Kinsu. Are you there?"

Kinsu sensed Mr. Knowlton standing over him while his classmates watched, but his eyes were still searching for the fluttering movements outside.

Alex looked up from his notebook, in which he had been doodling.

"Kinsu, come back to Earth!" Mr. Knowlton said. "Do you have the correct answer, or not?"

Snapping back, Kinsu not only gave the right answer but began spitting out other formulas and theories, confirming he was correct.

The class stared Kinsu down in amazement.

"Wow, okay, you ate your Wheaties today. Great job, Kinsu." Mr. Knowlton scratched through his wild hair. "You get a ten-point lead on the next test, which is... tomorrow, people."

And with this bit of bad news, the students had a second distraction on which to dwell, and therefore settled down.

In an attempt to hide his surprise, Mr. Knowlton made his way back to his desk. *That's curious. A breakthrough with scientific literacy from Kinsu? Something must be up.*

Alex, Jordan, and Rhee looked at Kinsu, then at each other. As best friends, they knew each other well and sensed something strange about one of their own.

Rhee tapped his head, gesturing to Kinsu how large his brain had become. But with Mr. Knowlton within earshot, even whispering was not an option. "What's up with that?" he mouthed, wiggling his thumbs, motioning for Kinsu to text him about what was up.

Kinsu shrugged as though he didn't quite know. Slumped in his chair, he took a moment to refocus, waiting for the bell. He watched the minute hand of the clock inch forward until the bell finally sounded.

The students rushed out the door.

"Hey, genius, where'd that come from?" Jordan used the back of his hand to check Kinsu's forehead for a fever. "Well, you're not hot. Was it the head-smack in the doorway that shook your brain?"

"You know I need a science tutor." Rhee looked bewildered. "You've been holding out on me, Kinsu?"

Alex chimed in. "What were you looking at out there? Mr. Knowlton must have called you, like, ten times, and it's like you didn't even hear him."

"I think I saw something," Kinsu said, rubbing his eyes. "Like someone walking really fast."

"In the trees?" Alex pointed toward the greenery in the distance. "What, you mean, like, campers?"

"No, there was, like, someone moving around or walking on the road. I can't explain it. I'm kind of tired. Maybe I was dreaming."

"Your eyes were open, Kinsu," Alex said. "You saw the road past the forest? I don't think so. The city is north so there are roads in that direction, but they are way too far for you to see them."

Void of resolution, the boys stood facing each other, acknowledging Kinsu must have seen something, but what it was they did not know.

Kinsu put on his headphones. He slapped Alex on the shoulder as the beat carried him to another class. "Later."

Rhee threw his hands in the air. "First, aqua boy, and now, campers in the trees. What's next?"

༄

Across campus during lunch, Josie sat beneath a tree on a freshly manicured lawn. Her long hair framed her pretty face, graced with pink lipstick and the perfect touch of makeup on her green eyes.

Alex came up from behind, touching her hand. "Do you ever think about going away after high school? With graduation coming up, we should consider all our options."

"Going where?" Josie snuggled close to him as he joined her under the tree.

"I mean, to a new city, to see more of the country. Like, more of the world."

"Well, I guess I have thought of it. Why?"

"I'll be an architect one day. You're interested in design. We should start our own firm when the time is right."

*Wow, a big thinker!* Josie smiled at the thought. "Sounds good, Alex. I've already been looking at some colleges. We should check out some new ones."

Alex took a slender, leather-bound book out of his backpack. "My sketchbook is getting full. I have some new office building designs in mind."

Josie touched the pages. "Your sketches are awesome."

"Thanks, babe. Just thinking out loud, that's all. Anyway, whether here or somewhere else, I just want you in the picture," Alex said.

Josie's cheeks grew warm. "Me too."

He kissed her lips softly.

Alex stared across the red brick campus, dreaming of the excitement he and Josie would find upon leaving Danville Heights.

❧

Coach Thomas was still fit and boyishly handsome in his early fifties. His gray temples, a sign of his years of experience, enhanced his appeal as a coach and mentor. Danville Heights High School had been his stomping ground, too.

A legend with vast experience as a quarterback, he carried a solid presence, earning the respect of the team and the community.

During practice, the field bustled as the business of molding soldiers for battle got underway.

"Listen up." Coach signaled to teammates across the field to gather and pay attention. "You must memorize all of the plays. Our reputation depends on it. The big game against Markley High School is right around the corner. We'll only have one shot at winning the war!"

The team headed back to the locker room. Coach huddled them together for one last pep talk. He preached a critical subject as he looked each player in the eye.

"If you think you'll be out there by yourself, think again. We're a team, and the bonds of kinship are in you. Remember, loyalty to the cause!" Coach went face-to-face with the players. "I have faith in you men. Let's show them what we're made of!"

Shortly after dismissal, the players scattered, gathering in small, chatty clusters. As Jordan, Rhee, and Kinsu dressed, they gave each other looks only best friends could interpret. They communicated through a sense of brotherhood that defied words, meaning—*we can do this*. Their bonds were indeed intertwined, strong enough to never be broken.

*Jordan, Rhee, Ronald, and Kinsu reassured each other through warrior-like glances, being careful not to lose the composure they would need for the ensuing battle against Markley High School.*

# Eight
## *Go Home Markley*

I N SMALL TOWNS, sports might be compared to fast-acting glue—a substance that holds things together no matter the conditions. Like a bonding agent, a baseball or football game can spark solidarity amongst locals on behalf of the town's players, especially the Danville Heights Chargers.

Tonight's game was against the Markley Lions, a winning team with top talent. Entire families came out to see the action, and the stadium was packed. This season, both teams had been undefeated. The winner would be the regional champion.

᭡

Coach Thomas swung the locker room door open. "Men, this is it. For some of you, this will be your last game wearing a Chargers uniform. Running onto that field representing your school will end tonight."

The team, in their maroon and gold uniforms, greeted him with bowed heads, holding tight to Coach's wisdom. It all came down to this one night.

"I'll be damned if we do not walk away from tonight with a trophy in our hands," Coach said.

Anxious players gripped their helmets.

Kinsu raised his head. His eyes shifted to Rhee and Jordan. Both were stone-faced as they hung on to Coach's words.

Coach moved closer to the players. "Now, we are going out there to play Chargers football."

The team responded in unison. "Yes, sir!"

"I can't hear you!"

"Yes, sir!"

The players stood together, ready to go to war.

Coach looked deep into Kinsu's eyes. "Quarterback, take us out to the field."

Jordan, Rhee, Ronald, and Kinsu reassured each other through warrior-like glances, being careful not to lose the composure they would need for the ensuing battle against Markley High School.

§

"Look at these houses, all pretty and perfect," Omar said. Under strict orders, mayhem had laced its shoes and marched right into Danville Heights.

"I don't get why *he* wants us to check out the place. Why can't we just grab and go?" asked the thug riding shotgun in Omar's stolen car, lint stuck to his hair.

"Don't ask stupid questions," Omar replied, looking out at the pristine porches.

They canvassed the empty streets of Danville Heights, noting the town's layout for Druth's takeover map. The roar of the football game was not far away.

"Is that what I think it is?" Omar slowed the car to a halt. "They got games, too? C'mon, let's check it out."

The thug grinned from ear to ear, peeping in on the action. "Wow!"

A few minutes passed. "Let's go." Omar glanced toward the quiet streets. "This ain't gonna last forever."

The wheels of his ride cranked forward.

Checking homes for unlocked gates and cracked windows, they found unsecured entry points along the entire block. Omar slid a window open, and they jumped inside.

"Druth said we may be in Danville for a while." Omar fluffed pillows on a couch. "So we'd better get comfy."

"Comfy would be good for a change," the thug said.

"Yeah, like house slippers and a cigar comfy."

"Hah... forget the TV, where's the bathrobe?"

And while the town was at the football game, sick laughter filled the air inside an empty home in Danville Heights.

❧

The referee blew his whistle for the coin flip.

Kinsu, Rhee, Jordan, and Ronald went out to the 50-yard line. From the opposite sideline, four huge-looking Lions, led by linebacker Sy Maddison, made their way across the field.

Sy was a solid beast of a human, easily 250 pounds of pure muscle. An NFL junkie, he looked like he was born out of a video game with full lips that never parted except to intimidate others or to stuff his face.

"Hey, boys, let's have a good game, all right?" The referee flipped the coin. "Call it in the air."

The coin twisted, flinging its fate above their heads.

Jordan could see a light swirling high above the coin.

Sy called it while staring at Kinsu. "Heads."

"Heads it is," the referee said. "What do you want to do?"

Sy adjusted his helmet. "We'll kick."

The referee nodded. "Okay, boys, out you go."

The players settled down and got into position.

Kinsu controlled the first possession of the game. He kept the momentum going inside the huddle. "Good start, guys. Let's keep it moving!"

But eventually, Sy's sheer power hammered the ball loose from his hands, knocking him down. *Dang, man! A fumble on the second possession of the game.*

Sy recovered the ball at the 40-yard line but was brought down quickly. He scrambled to his feet. "Didn't I tell you it was done? All day, baby!" he barked over a motionless Kinsu. "Might as well lay there for the rest of the game."

Kinsu was slow to get up and jog off the field. "We need to get the ball back," he said, shaking off the daze. "Rhee, you need to block Sy."

"Hey, it's not as easy as it looks!" Rhee snapped.

"Okay, calm down. It's still zero to zero." Ronald tried to quell the brewing storm. "It's early in the game. Let's tighten up."

The Lions took a seven-point lead, grinding it out to the goal line before punching into the end zone.

The Chargers needed to regroup, but at least Sy 'the Beast' was finally blocked by two Chargers linemen, including Rhee. The team kept pushing, each time harder than the last.

"Remember… loyalty to the cause!" Jordan said.

Third and fifteen, Kinsu air-mailed the ball. Ronald was down the sideline hustling for the pigskin, but the ball tipped off his fingertips, right into the hands of a Lions defender.

An interception. It was the Lions' ball.

Kinsu slammed his helmet on the bench. "You've got to be kidding me!" Teammates gathered around him.

"It happens, kid, hang in there," Coach Thomas said.

"Not tonight. It wasn't supposed to go like this. You should have caught it, Ronald!" Kinsu shouted.

Ronald sounded confused. "What?"

"If you could touch it, you could catch it."

Ronald looked displeased with his quarterback. "Oh, come on, man."

"Leadership... teamwork, Kinsu," Coach said.

The Lions controlled the ball. With thirteen seconds left in the half, they scored again.

Kinsu was beside himself. *Dang, fourteen to nothing. They're kicking our butts!*

❧

"And what are they doing, exactly?" Chase tilted his head sideways. His lips followed suit. "They need to pick it up. C'mon guys!"

Alex snacked on caramel peanuts. "Seriously, man. I would hate for my last game to end this way." He looked onto the field from high up in the stands.

"Last game?" Chase said.

Alex dug into the carton, picking up bits of hardened caramel with his finger. "Yeah, after high school, Josie and I will be going away to college... moving away from Danville Heights." He jammed twelve peanuts into his mouth. "You know... college, careers."

"Really? I didn't know that." Chase stared at Alex as the murmur of the game melted into the background. "We've been tight for so long. It would be weird without you, but I guess that's life."

"You have dreams of playing college baseball, which could lead to the pros. You're only one year behind me," Alex said. "You might be the next one to leave."

Chase raised his eyebrow. "That's true."

"The more I sketch, the better chance I'll have at becoming an architect. And Josie is a great designer. We're working on our plans, anyway." Alex bumped Chase with his shoulder. "Don't get all teary on me, bro. We'll always be tight. All of us."

Chase smiled. "Yeah, most def—"

A mass in the sky caught their attention. Something substantial with a bright center and feathered edges hovered for a few seconds, then faded away as though it had been discovered by the two.

"Speaking of weird," Chase said, "what was that?"

Holding his eighth handful of peanuts, Alex looked into the sky. "No words, dude. No words."

*The ball was released in the nick of time. As it flew through the air, the crowd was transfixed, their saucer-like eyes and gaped mouths on full display.*

# Nine

## *A Sad Trajectory*

CONTINUING ON THIS SAD TRAJECTORY, the Chargers received the kick, running until the clock ran out to halftime. The once boisterous crowd was still hopeful, but now basically silent as the Chargers trailed by two touchdowns, and on home turf at that.

Inside the locker room, a somber mood controlled the atmosphere. High schoolers with drooped heads accepting defeat. A sad sight indeed. Coach Thomas grabbed a black marker and wrote a single word on the board—Resilience. But the players did not see it.

"Let me tell you something about life," Coach said. "Sometimes, you'll be down. The help you thought you had vanishes. You think your world has ended. Listen, you will only survive through faith and resilience.

"Now, if every game was done after the first half, then fine, we can pack it in. But, there are two more quarters to play. This game is only half-way over. There's still time on the clock. Men, we can do this!"

The players perked up. Teammates glanced around, nodding to each other.

"Now, let's go out there and shut them down." Coach went over the plays, then slammed the playbook against a locker. "Let's go make history!"

The team felt a sense of rejuvenation after Coach's words, sprinting back out onto the field. One by one, they tapped the 'Chargers Pride' sign above the door.

Even if they couldn't come back in this game, they were surely going down swinging.

❧

A jewelry box turned upside down. Scattered possessions, stolen checks. Omar and the thug made their way through rooms, filling their bags with loot.

"Got me a new computer, see." Omar fit a laptop snugly beneath his arm.

"Good for you." The thug looked around for something to eat. "Where's the food?"

On the next block, Mrs. Perkins, who was too tired to go to the football game, prepared for a stroll while all was quiet. Down the way, a police cruiser revved its engine to begin its nightly patrol.

"Let's get this stuff in the car," Omar said.

Hunger pangs spoke to the thug. "Hang on, I got hands on an apple."

"I said, c'mon, dummy!"

In the rush to get the loot into the trunk, Omar accidentally tore off a section of the takeover map, which floated to the sidewalk. He turned the engine on. Nasty gunk sputtered from the car as it swerved from side to side, creating waves of dust.

The hooligan palmed the shiny, red apple and sank his teeth into it. "Juicy!"

Heading north toward the dark city of Sandry Lake, they turned a corner, driving right past the Danville Heights police officer on patrol.

"Sit back and be cool. Don't make any moves." Omar ducked down in his seat. "Don't even bite that stupid apple."

The thug replied through stuffed lips. "Roger that."

The officer followed the vehicle to the edge of his jurisdiction. He pulled over, stepped out of his cruiser, and stared the car down until it was out of sight.

❧

Kinsu and his offensive squad had waited for their turn to get back onto the field. With the snap, he faked a handoff to his running back, Jordan, and kept possession of the ball. As he began to throw, his eyesight went fuzzy, then came back extra sharp.

71

A bright light raced across the sky, but Kinsu had no time to process the glowing streak.

Ronald was wide open, far down the field. Kinsu threw a deep pass. Ronald caught it and ran 53 yards.

A sweet chorus of claps swept the stadium.

Coach called the next play. "Jordan, you take the handoff."

"Got it, Coach!" Jordan took the handoff and raced around the right end, then cut for the end zone. The only person between him and the goal was Sy 'the Beast'. He ran toward Sy, spun, eluded the tackle, and dove into the end zone for the touchdown. *Yes! Take that, Michelin Man.*

Down by only one touchdown, the team had found their groove, and so did their loyal fans.

The players stayed focused into the third quarter with just a few minutes left on the clock. And with the snap, the ball was thrown to the wrong route, hitting the dirt, forcing the Lions to punt the ball.

With the clock ticking louder, time seemed to evaporate, forcing both teams to contemplate their strategies. Early in the fourth quarter battle, they had traded possession of the ball multiple times without either scoring.

"That's okay, men, stay the course," Coach said, trying to keep the team motivated. "Remember the plays. Brotherhood! Teamwork!"

With three minutes left in the game, the Chargers had the ball, still down by seven. They pushed up the field, battling Sy, the defense, and the clock. Before they knew it, only twenty-four seconds remained.

Coach used his final timeout, stopping the clock at nineteen seconds. "Sy will try to rush Kinsu, so you need to get the ball off quick. Okay? Let's go!"

When the ball was snapped, Sy dove at Kinsu, trying to tackle him, but it was released in the nick of time. As it flew through the air, the crowd was transfixed, their saucer-like eyes and gaped mouths on full display.

Ten seconds remained.

Ronald caught the ball, straight arming a defender, running into the end zone for a touchdown. The crowd's joyful screams filled the air.

The Chargers were one point away from sending the game into overtime.

❧

Mrs. Perkins took pleasure in a quiet, leisurely walk. *Just lovely*, she thought. Strolling along, she noticed something beneath her feet. *A piece of paper? Looks like part of a map.* She picked it up and held it to her nose. *Not from around these parts.*

A small, bouncing light ball greeted her. She clicked her tongue. It came closer to her. She held the piece of paper in front of it. One more click and it sped high into the sky.

The patrol officer spotted Mrs. Perkins. He cruised over to her, stopped his car, and leaned out the window. "Hello, ma'am."

"Good evening, officer. Look what fell from the sky."

"Used to be a lucky penny. Now, it's part of a map?" he said. "Those squiggly lines look like the river. And this part here... a road leading to Lavender Quarry?"

Mrs. Perkins glanced skyward. "Peculiar, indeed."

ఞ

The stunned crowd reverted to its silent mode, their fingers digging into the edges of their seats.

During the huddle, the mood was set.

The kicker made his way onto the field.

Both teams were on the line.

The defense reared its ugly head with mean grunts carrying warnings of a blocked kick. Kinsu stayed in sync with the agreement in the huddle—going for a two-point conversion.

Snap went the ball, and the players went to war. Pads smashed and players yelled. It was down to one final play.

The kicker planted his eye firmly on the ball. He arched back, then ran forward with great speed, but veered sharply to the right, purposely missing the ball.

The crowd's vision of the ball gliding toward the goal post had sailed into nowhere land, as Kinsu, the holder for the point after, grabbed the ball, darting to the left.

The defense charged their way through the line.

With Sy right upon Kinsu's neck, Rhee rushed over, mustering every ounce of his strength, and blocked Sy before he could get his hands on Kinsu.

In a mad scramble, Kinsu eluded the furious pursuit of the defense, shooting to the right with his eye on Ronald.

Kinsu fired a bullet pass to the 1-yard line where Ronald jumped, made a spectacular catch, and flipped himself backward into the end zone as the final second made itself known to the crowd.

Cheers erupted from the stands.

The trick play worked! The Chargers defied the odds and won the game. Fans, cheerleaders, and the rest of the team stormed the field.

Coach rushed over to Kinsu. "One heck of a play, kid!" He hugged him on the greatest day of their lives.

"Thanks for having faith in me, Coach," Kinsu said.

"Are you kidding me? You're amazing!"

Teammates passed the championship trophy as tiny lights twinkled in the sky. Chase and Alex ran from the bleachers and joined the celebration.

Chase rushed his friends, hugging whomever he could grab. "That was awesome!"

Alex fist-bumped Rhee. "Mad skills, guys."

Kinsu shared in the satisfaction of teamwork with Jordan and Rhee. "Guys, we did it!"

"Boys like brothers," Jordan said.

The five friends piled together, overlapping hands, chanting in unison, "Brothers forever!"

Jordan felt a body chill. He looked to the heavens, honoring his late mother, Talia, with the final play. *Miss you, Mom.*

The Chargers were the regional champions. Beaming with Danville pride, their hard-earned goal was finally complete.

*They observed dark, inviting paths sparkling beneath the moonlight. The friends were excited by the on-off-on of tiny, blinking lights in the night air, which looked like creative beings seeking new friends.*

# Ten

## *Fresh Emotion*

**W**ITH FRESH EMOTION, renewed spirit, and lingering satisfaction from a job well done, Kinsu, Rhee, and Jordan embarked upon a new adventure. Although their muscles had been overextended during the game, they paid them no mind as they ventured through the one place Danville Heights residents steered clear of—the forbidden preserve.

Before they set out, the boys had sent text messages to their families, reminding them Rhee was hosting the post-game party in his backyard studio. With their alibi established, they were all spending the night.

"Hey, guys, over here." Jordan led the way. "Let's check it out, just this one time."

They observed dark, inviting paths sparkling beneath the moonlight. The friends were excited by the on-off-on of tiny, blinking lights in the night air, which looked like creative beings seeking new friends.

Beautiful clicking noises filled the air. The strange sounds were charming, rhythmic, like pulsating clocks.

Jordan shuffled his feet to the music-like clacks. "You hear that?" He bounced his shoulders, his elbows at an angle.

Kinsu bobbed his head, feeling the vibe of the clicks. "If I can get that sound into one of my beats I'll win that contest for sure." He waved his hand through the air.

Chase and Alex, who were out of breath from running, soon joined the guys. The group basked in the relaxed melody of the sounds.

"Interesting," Chase said. "Maybe it isn't true what they say about this place."

"My dad broke it down to me one time. But who else said something about it?" Jordan asked.

"Well, according to rumors, some kind of violence happened in here years ago," Chase explained. "That's why no one ever comes to this place."

The forest cast a foreboding aura that proved to be a warning. However, its dark reputation stood in direct contrast with its natural appeal.

Huge, tropical plants with sprawling leaves blanketed the preserve. It was stunningly beautiful. In daylight, one could see an array of succulent greens offering a refreshing reprieve from a busy day.

At night, those greens became even more inviting, deep, and intimate. An interesting glimmer lit up the forest with a beckoning glow.

Alex studied the clicking noises, remembering the rumors they'd heard about the preserve, and what their parents had told them about it. *Just because we won the game, there's no reason to not believe our parents.* He peered over his shoulder, turning slowly. "Hey, guys, are you sure about this?"

The other four were ready to explore.

"Yeah, we're sure." Jordan maintained his stride. "Why, what's up?"

Alex stopped walking to observe this new, dramatic environment. His parents' voices echoed inside his head. For a moment, he considered turning around but realized he was alone. His friends had picked up the pace and were nearly out of sight.

Against his better judgment, he charged ahead, paying attention to the clacking symphony, which distracted him from his concerns.

As they continued through the preserve, each of the boys observed the trees and plants with full wonder, noticing the captivating curves of the leaves.

Kinsu was sure he had seen these beautifully bent lines before. "I think I remember something," he told the group. "My brother and I were chasing a jackrabbit when we were little. It was hopping so fast, running all over. We were laughing our heads off. We took off after it...

straight toward the forest. We were sure we could catch it."

"Uh-oh, was your dad around?" Rhee asked. "Belt time."

"Yeah, that's just it. When Dad saw us, he was frantic. He ran after us like crazy. My mom was trying to keep up as fast as she could. I'm not sure, but I think she was crying."

Rhee stared at the blinking lights above their heads. "So, what happened?"

"Dad yelled for us to stop, but we just kept running."

Kinsu thought back to the event. He could remember his father, Juson, watching him and his brother run toward the preserve, and how he took off after them.

He recalled his mother, Della, shaking in distress, her hand gripping her chest as she had shouted to his father to get them out of there.

Kinsu patted his behind. "My dad threatened us with a spanking if we didn't come back."

Chastened, the boys had finally slowed down.

"The jackrabbit raced ahead and out of sight. We lost it!" Kinsu said, his arms up in the air. "Dad caught up to us and told us to never go into the forest. He said it was dark in there and we would get lost."

Kinsu recalled Juson's black hair glistening in the sun, the bright light sharpening his features. "I remember seeing a tear in my dad's eye."

A tear that was so artfully curved at the bottom.

When Kinsu had looked past his father and into the edge of the forest, he saw that same curve on a brilliant leaf waving around in the distance.

Kinsu had seen his mother shaking, battling what he didn't know were violent memories of the night she and Juson had been trapped in a dark hell, overhearing a vicious murder in the preserve some years back.

Rhee was stone-faced, totally sucked into Kinsu's story. "What did your mom say?"

"Nothing." Kinsu was still unsure why his mother was so upset. "But she was crying her eyes out."

"Wow, that gave me a chill," Alex said, wrapping his arms around himself. "I wondered why we weren't allowed to come in here."

Because of the emotion of Kinsu's story, Chase saw the need to lighten the mood. He struck up an animated discussion about the night's big game. "Hey, guys, check it out. That long pass in the fourth quarter put Markley on notice." His outstretched arm reenacted a move from the field.

"Yeah, Sy Maddison just stood there, blinking," Kinsu said, pulling himself out of the memories. "But by then, we were so charged. It was like a gladiator pit. Just crazy!"

"Now look, men. I want one thousand squats, right now!" Jordan walked around, imitating Coach Thomas. "If you want to beat Markley, you have to do what cavemen did to defend themselves against dinosaurs. You have to get focused and strong. You have to go the extra mile like you're being chased for your lives! Now, get out there and challenge yourselves to become better warriors. And give me five hundred push-ups, too!"

Jordan sounded just like Coach Thomas, a fearsome former player, and an even more intimidating coach.

Rhee and Kinsu laughed, holding their stomachs, trying to control their buckling knees.

Tears streamed across Rhee's face. "Seriously!"

"One more push-up and I'll quit the team," Kinsu said, leaning against a tree, still clutching his stomach.

As their laughter subsided, they began to stride with purpose. The crunch of fallen leaves under their feet made for lasting memories as the five friends pushed ahead, deep into the emerald glow of the preserve.

*The being's creativity advanced in a display of twirls and spins, astonishing the boys. And they followed their little friend further and further into the forest.*

# Eleven
## *Mixed and Mashed*

A S ONE WOULD IMAGINE, a mysterious forest might offer deep, eerie chills, especially at night. Instead, the forest cast a rich glow, and the environment was beautiful and serene.

Walking slowly with their eyes absolutely feasting on the horticultural delights, the boys were approached by something they weren't sure was real. It floated effortlessly, lighting up in a sporadic pattern, but had neither sound nor discernible shape, other than being somewhat clear and round.

Its fluttering wings suspended it in the center of their disbelieving huddle. All eyes were on it, but what it was provoked more mystery than the forest itself. It bounced in a cheery, beckoning fashion, flashing its stunning wings, drawing the boys into a never-ending waltz. They were transfixed, unable to glance at each other, prevented by the daze each silently battled.

The little glowing being carried about, moving closer to their faces. It moved in and out of trees, spewing sparkle and splendor, then floated away from the boys, yet stayed close enough to continue the enticement.

Contributing to the amazing glow ricocheting from sprawling fronds to soaring trees and fallen leaves, the being's creativity advanced in a display of twirls and spins, astonishing the boys. And they followed their little friend further and further into the forest.

Deeper ahead, the visual spectacle beautifully intertwined with the clicking noise, which grew louder and more defined, moving up the scale into high notes. The repetition of the noise mesmerized the boys, equating to an invisible lasso.

The friends grouped together, looking ahead and behind. Their stomachs tightened as the tension grew.

What they saw next would pale in comparison to their little, wondrous friend, who steadily bounced around several curvy pathways.

The small creature led them into an area deep within the preserve housing two large, floating, clicking balls of light. The boys instinctively covered their eyes, yet still tried to peep through their fingers.

The light balls began spinning wildly and grew louder, with their tops spitting out free-falling shavings of light like fireworks.

The sputtering light bounced off the dirt only to end up against a tree or one of the boys, then back down and up again.

Slowing down, the beings moved in between the boys. Too scared to move and struggling with reality, the boys' eyes locked onto the radiant balls.

And with a striking force, the five friends were encased by a bright, piercing light as the balls exploded, emitting their energy onto the boys.

Mixing and mashing north, south, east, and west, bright waves covered the soil, spreading across trees, rock, and all plant life. The forest fell silent, frozen like an inhale without an exhale. It was dark and quiet, except for the liquid energy dripping from the huge, wavy leaves.

Being subjected to drifts both in and out of reality, the boys succumbed to the lure of a vacant black space within the deepest parts of their minds. They fell to the ground unconscious, laying in this forbidden domain in the center of a place they had been warned not to approach.

And from some distance toward the other side of the preserve, a draped shadow had been looking inward and saw this mysterious incident.

The curve of his black hood was loose enough for him to witness the unthinkable. But it also shrouded his expression, which was impassive.

This figure, a dark stranger, had been watching the boys for a period of time and saw the explosion of light. He knew it had exposed them to a grave risk in this place of both awe and fear. He realized time would now take the reins as a master guide for these stricken young men, all of whom would need hope as a rod and stamina as a spear on the long journey ahead.

Knowing the veil of normalcy would need to be maintained in order for this inconceivable episode to be minimized, the Dark Stranger drew upon his strength to physically move each of the boys to Rhee's house.

He knew familiar surroundings would ease them as they roused, barely able to comprehend their predicament.

For he knew much, and every step, every footprint left an indelible impression on the path leading to the studio in Rhee's backyard. Indeed, footprints providing a window to the past meshed with hope for the future.

And like a laser, the Dark Stranger steadied his gait, hurling each one up and over his powerful shoulders.

As he absorbed the totality of the scene, he breathed deeply. His head hung in a manner to which only trauma could relate. But in a sign of resilience it swiftly sprung back.

Under the circumstances, he knew time would not be patient nor friendly.

Welcome or unwelcome.

Fate had arrived.

*Haze hovered like a low-flying plane just cruising above the surface. Going nowhere, it had no landing strategy and no real direction. The boys had been in a deep slumber and they were all feeling battered, tired, and drained.*

# Twelve
## *Tired and Drained*

A S IT INCHED ITS WAY across Danville Heights, the sun met the treetops in a spirited manner, suggesting it was time to play. Birds sang in harmony. Mrs. Perkins rocked slowly. Dew bid farewell in its customary fashion while the emerald blades guarded yet another secret.

It was Saturday morning, and the town was due to stir. Not to be missed, however, was a lingering glow deep within the preserve. Nearly undetectable by morning, there was no doubt the forest understood the meaning of déjà vu.

After a while, a lawn mower roared close to the studio where the boys were sleeping. Finally, they woke, getting their first view of the day, which was nothing more than them staring at each other.

Barely moving about in a confused state, each found himself in the throes of an unpleasant, subtle agony. Throbbing soreness stung their bodies.

Jordan shifted his head, trying to shake the loud ringing in his ears. Despite pushing against his head, the noise refused to vacate.

Alex was too foggy to move. He lay there licking his lips, which only made them drier by the minute. His tongue separated from the roof of his mouth with a loud smack, begging to be quenched. A sore throat made matters worse.

A dense fog welcomed Kinsu, as hazy, smoggy vision moved in. Like melted fog, dew clouded his eyes.

Across the room, Chase battled stinging, cold hands that felt odd in the middle of a warm fall.

Blood dripped from Rhee's nose. He stood up but was unsteady on his feet.

Bizarre ailments stacked against the boys, leaving them slow to move through physical pain.

"We played against Markley last night, right?" Alex said, recalling the big game.

"Yeah, at least I remember that." Rhee threw his head back to stem the flow of blood. "Somebody get me a tissue."

"Put some pressure on it." Kinsu was unsure if Rhee was Rhee… or Jordan… or Alex, who all looked blurry. "Squeeze it, you know, like your mom would do."

"We just woke up," Chase said, "but I'm ready to go back to sleep."

Haze hovered like a low-flying plane just cruising above the surface. Going nowhere, it had no landing strategy and no real direction. The boys had been in a deep slumber and they were all feeling battered, tired, and drained.

Regardless, the day would not wait.

"Let's go inside." Rhee grabbed a crumpled t-shirt to plug his nose as he peeped through the window. "I'm pretty sure my mom's wondering if we're still alive."

The five friends mustered the strength to move.

Rhee opened the sliding glass door as they arrived to the kitchen. Traveling smoothly along the tracks, at least its left-to-right direction was predictable within a strange and uncertain morning.

Jordan whiffed an aroma from the warming drawer. "I may not feel good, but there's nothing wrong with my appetite." He searched for a seat at the counter.

Rhee wondered what his mom had whipped up this time. "She did it again."

Rhee's single mother, Sandy Smith, worked as a teller for the town's only bank—Danville Heights Central Union Bank. Her culinary masterpieces spoke to her love of gardening. She ran a tight ship, doing everything a mother and father would have done. Her style involved authoritative delegation, and she didn't play.

Rhee knew the drill all too well. If Sandy ever came home to find a mess had been left for her, there were sure to be issues.

"These are the best breakfast burritos I've ever had. Like... ever," Kinsu mumbled, barely audible through the layers of food he had shoved into his mouth.

"No kidding," Chase agreed, stretching out on the loveseat across from the bar. "I'll take the leftovers."

Persistent thirst chased Alex. "That looks so good." Sandy's freshly squeezed orange juice, garnished with mint from her garden, stood on the counter placing him in a trance. He lunged for the juice, spilling it. "Oops," he said, guzzling the remains.

"Wait a minute. It's all gone?" Jordan watched the juice vanish. "You okay, dude?"

Alex smacked his lips, looking around for more. "Just thirsty."

Jordan examined his own empty glass. "Oh, okay... no worries, bro."

"Here guys, have at it." Rhee shared some apple juice from the fridge.

Sandy entered the room, curious to see how things were with the boys. "Good afternoon."

Stuffed mouths greeted her. "Hi, Ms. Smith."

Her light brown tresses flowed with a silky ripple showing waves with all natural end curls. She was a physically fit woman who understood the need to balance life's pressures with her own well-being. With the signs of a stressful divorce no longer showing, she lived life fully.

"Hey, Mom, thanks for the chow," Rhee said.

"Of course. I knew you all would be hungry after that fantastic finish last night." She studied each of the boys and their companion lethargy. "You must be tired from the game. You guys were out like a light."

"Yeah, we were seriously tired," Rhee said.

"Is that blood on your nose?" Sandy asked.

"Oh, it's nothing." Rhee did his best to play it off. "Must've been too hot under the blanket last night."

"Let me see." Sandy tilted Rhee's head.

"I'm okay, Mom. See, it stopped already. I'm fine."

The guys listened to the exchange between Sandy and Rhee, hoping they weren't next.

"Okay, but let me know if it starts bleeding again." She turned her attention to Kinsu, who was continuously rubbing his eyes. "Did you get hit in the eye last night, Kinsu?" She swept his hair to the side.

"No, but it was hard to see at one point," Kinsu said.

"We have plenty of eye drops in the cabinet if you need them."

"Okay, thank you, Ms. Smith." Despite his vision moving in and out of sharpness, Kinsu captured her graceful demeanor as she conversed in her usual motherly fashion.

Being the intuitive creature she was, the fatigue issue bothered her. "Were you boys up real late?"

"Not really. Well, maybe," Alex said through chapped lips.

"Well, Saturday's almost half gone, so you guys eat, clean up, and enjoy the sunshine while you can." She exited the room in total observation of the sluggish brigade.

Her final glance landed upon Alex, whose desperate quest of the last drop of that minty-orange goodness continued feverishly, and in plain view.

*His nose burned. A river of tears cooled the pain. Something ran by, but looking at it tore into his sight. Swirling waves of angry light brought rebuke.*

# Thirteen

## *A New Obsession*

DRUTH WRESTLED with a bunched up pillow on an uncomfortable bed. A numb left arm also messed with his sleep. When he turned over, he finally fell into a deep slumber. With an intermix of dark images and bright layers swirling in his dreams, an insatiable desire crept around, finally making its way to the other side.

And deeper, he drifted away.

Bearing in mind the hearty tugs of aroma and taste, he licked his fingers while walking aimlessly, hearing echoes, and searching for someone.

Overactive saliva glands became a chore, and he struggled to keep from choking, using his sleeves to catch the mess. Hunger and thirst chased him down. Shadows pursued him in the night, causing him to wonder, *Where am I?*

Fragrances shot out of the dark, fiercely competing for his attention. All kinds, all scents, impossible to choose only one. His nose burned. A river of tears cooled the pain.

Something ran by, but looking at it tore into his sight. Swirling waves of angry light brought rebuke.

Even still, his nature would not be denied in the hostile fog. "I will find you!" he shouted.

The stinging scent of rotting anger exploded into showers. He took cover, but upon opening his eyes, a bright light confronted him, clicking in his ear. Intense heat overtook him, and he faded into the darkness.

And a panicked Druth woke up in a horrible sweat.

Probing himself for what he now thought was missing, his senses burned as he suspected someone else had the gifts. "What's going on? Something must have happened. I'm going to find you!"

And in an instant, Druth's obsession with finding the gifts had forged its way into his mind, adding to the web of confusion in the dark city of Sandry Lake.

*With their belongings collected, Alex, Kinsu, Chase, and Jordan went their way, back to their homes, carrying with them a greater sense of connection to each other.*

# Fourteen

## *Soapy Water*

A S THE MINUTES PRESSED FORWARD, Chase and Alex exchanged glances filled with a sense of knowing something. But what? After they caught up with the others on the walk last night, an incident occurred, but distorted thoughts made it hard to remember.

After the meal at Rhee's house, Jordan heard a peculiar noise. "Rhee, are you expecting company? Someone's outside."

Rhee slid out of his chair. "Not that I know of."

Jordan pressed against the window and saw a squirrel in a tree. Its movements rang incredibly loud in his ears. "What! A tiny animal?"

Walking backward from the window, he winced, covering his ears. The sound of the squirrel's scamper shook Jordan, causing him to trip, nearly breaking one of Sandy's blown glass vases.

"Hey, watch out!" Rhee made a mad dash to save his mother's vase. "What the heck just happened?"

An embarrassed Jordan picked himself up from the floor. "I could hear the squirrel right inside my head."

"That's weird, because I smelled something." Rhee looked out the window to be sure the squirrel was the only visitor. "It was like... pine or something."

Jordan held his head. "I can't believe that. What's going on?"

"Man, I really don't know," Rhee said.

A subtle unease struck the group as they prepared to go their separate ways.

"It's getting late. We'd better get going." Chase stuffed his phone into his backpack. "I've got chores today, Sunday will fly by, then here comes school on Monday."

With their belongings collected, Alex, Kinsu, Chase, and Jordan went their way, back to their homes, carrying with them a greater sense of connection to each other.

಄

Familiar pathways brought a sense of calm to the group as they walked home.

"At least we know one thing. We beat the heck out of Markley." Alex pumped his fist. "Well, at the end of the game, anyway."

Chase recalled a girl with a high ponytail. "Yeah, and the cheerleaders were fine, too."

"Markley's got a good team," Kinsu said. "They just need to quit scrunching up their faces and looking so mad all the time, especially Sy 'the Beast'!"

"Yeah, really! They should get some masks and stop scaring the poor fans," Chase said, his eyes bugged out, fake biting his nails in horror.

"Tired or not, yardwork awaits." Alex saw uneven edges on the lawn at his house. "No escaping that one." His little brother and sister burst out the front door, jumping and screaming for their big brother. "Later, guys." He swept the kids back inside, disappearing behind the frosty glass door.

Chase, Kinsu, and Jordan started feeling like themselves again. A warm breeze refreshed the group.

"My mom's birthday is coming up." Jordan reflected on his mother's exuberance. "She loved big parties. We still celebrate her birthday, cake and all."

"Really? That's so cool," Kinsu said.

"Yeah, I really miss my mom." Jordan reflected warmly. "But I still can't believe she was drinking and driving. Sometimes, I wonder if that was true."

"Her death was really hard on my family, too." Kinsu placed his hand on Jordan's shoulder. "She and my mom were good friends."

"We're still sorry for your loss, Jordan," Chase said.

Jordan nodded. "Thanks, man, we appreciate it."

The friends moved further down the block. At Chase's house, they saw Diane washing her car in the driveway, smacking water beads with a fluffy towel.

"She's helping with my chores." Chase walked toward Diane with open arms. "What a great sister."

"You always did have excellent timing, Chase." Diane rolled a fresh towel into a ball. "Here's a dry one. Catch!"

Chase caught it mid-air. "Can't I go inside first?"

"Where have you been all morning? You're never this late."

"At Rhee's. Just hanging out."

The guys began to shuffle their feet.

Jordan dreaded his own Saturday chores. "I'm too tired to clean today."

He and Kinsu waved goodbye.

"Guess what? My essay was the favorite in my English class. I got an A+." Diane beamed, pumping glass cleaner on the window.

"Oh, that's awesome," Chase said. "It pays to study." He walked around her car checking to see if she had remembered to scrub the tires and rims.

"It sure does." Diane checked for streaks on the glass, then headed for the house. "I'll fix some lunch."

Chase rubbed his forearms and squeezed the tension out of his hands. He reached for a soapy rag inside a bucket. *Diane missed a couple of spots.* Water began to dance with his fingertips. Deep warmth moved up his arm as if it were growing hotter with each passing moment. "Ouch!"

He kicked the bucket sideways, causing soapy water to spill over his shoes. Oddly, he felt compelled to look north in the direction of... Sandry Lake.

Diane overheard Chase kicking the bucket. She stepped outside. "I saw Sandy last week," she said, playing it cool, surveying the mess as she approached her brother. "She said she was interested in going for a promotion on her job."

"Uh-huh," Chase mumbled, still gazing north.

Diane gathered the towels. "Did you see her while you were at Rhee's?"

"Uh-huh."

"Is everything okay?" Diane tried to show patience with Chase's teenage ways. "What are you looking at?"

"Nothing. I had a little accident." He pointed to the spilled water. "I'd better clean up." His squeaky shoes carried him toward the house.

Diane shook her head. "Well, at least the car is clean."

With the day in motion, she would try her best to get a few more chores out of her brother before too long, if she could keep him focused.

*Although the friends were bonded, the ambiguous nature of it all bore further examination. Yet what was missing was the guidebook needed to navigate these new and challenging waters.*

# Fifteen
## *Woven Fibers*

**B**ACK AT RHEE'S HOUSE, Sandy prepped her raised planting beds. She cleared things out to make way for the cover crops, and mulched the pathways. She glanced at the studio where the boys had been sleeping, giving it a long stare.

Her eyes beamed with suspicion. *I wonder if there was more to the story than they said.* She had noticed how tired they were and wasn't putting anything past them.

She went inside to inspect the quarters, sniffing pillows and looking behind the game console from the viewpoint of concern, but with a hint of wariness in case something turned up. *Were they smoking or drinking to celebrate the game?*

She flipped the pages of a magazine, spewing the lightest air flurries into her face, realizing the futility of her investigation, which led to nothing.

The garden called to her, so she proceeded to return to the raised beds, leaving the door ajar from where five sleepy boys had emerged, taking their first steps into unknown territory that hardly offered a clue as to what lies ahead.

એ

The sensations the boys were experiencing flowed like a river meandering through a wild countryside. From blurry to clear, achy to painful, the gamut had been realized.

But as the weekend progressed, there was also an inexplicable, silent connection emerging amongst the boys. Practically cryptic, their ability to sense each other caused guarded reactions so others would not see their expressions, which must have looked confused.

Although the friends were bonded, the ambiguous nature of it all bore further examination. Yet what was missing was the guidebook needed to navigate these new and challenging waters.

Even worse, the north continuously summoned while the five friends communicated through silent awareness.

એ

Alex puttered around doing his normal chores, sweeping away and such, with his two sidekicks in tow. Being the older brother, he was expected to lead by example, showing the kiddies that part of life's success lies in hard work. But lingering fatigue forced him to pause. He resumed his chores with intention, but felt weary and unfocused. And as the broom met the wall, he thought about Josie.

At the same time, a strange and immediate sense of his friends was evident. *Why do the guys keep popping into my head?*

He yawned, toughing it out, but behind the scenes, the alignment of their instincts for some common cause was brewing, as a mysterious course took shape.

&#8766;

Sheer, gold fabric with subtle hints of sparkle framed the window in Josie's bedroom. The sun cast a warm glow from where she was peeking out.

Like woven threads hugging each other to form a lasting connection, she and Alex had developed quite a bond. *I miss him. I wonder where he is.*

Saturday's routine normally included the two taking a walk, seeing a show, or just hanging out. With their meetup behind schedule, Josie was concerned.

After all, it was past midday and time to get a move on things. *Let me give him a call.* The phone rang into oblivion, so she canceled the line. *That's weird.*

Several blocks away, with the broom and the wall now in an extended meeting, Alex had given in to the fatigue that had been chasing him, and he fell asleep.

He never even heard his phone ring.

Sun shining, day moving, Josie met those woven fibers face-to-face, glancing through to see the lovely, natural surroundings looking the same as yesterday.

❧

A faint noise filled Jordan's ears, soft ripples floating in and out, twisting and twirling, lasting a few seconds, sounding like whispers or a muffled murmur. After a long pause, his fingers mingled with the big waves in his hair, and he looked to the north.

Hoping the noise would cease, he waited it out. He searched every thought since the game to elicit an ever-elusive answer to the nagging, audible intrusion.

*I have an idea... earplugs.* Jordan searched his room for a pair of plugs to stuff deep into his ears. *There they are. These might work.* He rolled the springy blue plugs between his fingers and inserted them into his ears.

The plugs silenced the world as they expanded, quieting the room.

He stood for a while, waiting for the noise to fade away, but it seemed to intensify, cutting right through the plugs.

Deeper than his ear space, his advanced audible perception had become innate, generating from within.

He ripped the plugs from his ears and threw them across the room. "No peace!"

From his home, Kinsu was also gazing north from time to time. His vision had played games, from sharp to blurry, and all in between.

Mysterious as it was, the lure of the north bore deep roots. It offered strange allure and a calling to seek its meaning, to unveil a tale locked away in the darkness.

The lines between confusion and destiny started to blur. Images behind an invisible curtain began to go dark. It seemed those northern shadows were coming alive, dark and distant, yet so close to the peaceful town of Danville Heights.

*Candlelight flickered in the Dark Stranger's eyes, illuminating his handsome, yet slightly worn face. His long hair trailed outside his hood as he shuffled photographs and newspaper clippings he had stored inside a tattered shoebox.*

## Sixteen
# *The Dark Stranger*

EXHIBITING AN UNUSUAL COMBINATION of heightened senses, the Dark Stranger was able to see, hear, and smell with incredible depth. He twisted the handle of the side door on his modest cottage—a place of guarded solitude. Inhaling a woodsy scent, his eyes swept through his dwelling.

*I need sleep. But it's hard to rest with a full mind*, he thought, as he stepped into the quarters. *I feel for those boys.* He knew indecision would soon give way to the tugs and pulls of life he, and the boys, would experience.

Abandoned long ago by early residents of Danville Heights, the tattered cottage, located just outside of town, served his needs. Rustic interiors defined the space. Neatly folded blankets sat atop a worn mattress cradled by plain black iron. A light hung from the center of the ceiling, casting shadows beneath a wooden table and chairs. He unfastened wide black sashes, loosening window coverings with dark flecks throughout, which hung from a metal rod.

His fingers slid between the grooves of the chair-back as he pulled it toward him, the legs scraping the floor before he sat. He struck a long-stemmed match, which touched a candle. The light flickered in his eyes, illuminating his handsome, yet slightly worn face. His long hair trailed outside his hood as he shuffled photographs and newspaper clippings he had stored inside a tattered shoebox.

An old photograph showed the Dark Stranger in his late teens posing with a similar-looking young man. Various images captured friends at parties and family gatherings. And curiously, there was a high school yearbook photo of Jordan's mother, Talia Platero.

He unfolded an aged newspaper article with a startling headline—'Missing Persons Report: Trail Gone Dead'—including a photograph of him and another young man. He felt a sense of deep despair as his mind regressed into old, painful memories.

He recalled seeing his mother crying her heart out as he stood looking through a window of his childhood home. His father had been unable to console her.

He remembered walking through the preserve with four others, hearing clicking noises among laughter and friendship. His mind took him to the edge of the preserve where huge, wavy leaves had danced in the night. His eyes had traced the leaves as they beckoned amongst blinking lights in the distance.

He studied a photograph of an old friend. *The weight of your passing has anchored me like a sunken ship. I should have been there to save you, to protect you. I'm sorry. Please forgive me.*

Although the memories had taken him to a dark place within his heart, the light from the candle offered the flecks of hope he would need to keep going. *Not to worry, friend. I will make it right one day.*

Channeling his pain into guiding the boys brought a heavy, reluctant sense of responsibility. But as the candle faded, final waves of concern faded with it sending outward and upward the strength needed to carry tomorrow forward.

*Triggering bitter memories, the loud clicking noises shook the Dark Stranger. He stepped boldly to uncover the mysterious intrusion.*

# Seventeen

## *The Nectar*

A MYSTERIOUS GLOW within the preserve illuminated the horticultural wonders. It was cast from the Naculeans who were in the midst hovering, accentuating the natural appeal of their earthly domain. Their impatience with what they knew was on the horizon could nearly be felt, and most certainly heard.

"Our mission must be fulfilled."

"It is chosen."

"The transition has begun."

"Time will not wait."

"We must empower the others."

"He must be stopped."

"It is chosen."

Loud clicks rang out in the preserve.

"That noise! Who's there?" the Dark Stranger shouted, his fingers curling, tightening. He had left his cottage and was inside the preserve reflecting upon the boys' predicament, and searching for the answers to life.

Triggering bitter memories, the loud clicking noises shook him. "I said... who's there?" He stepped boldly to uncover the mysterious intrusion.

A decipherable version of the clicking emerged to facilitate an exchange.

"We are with you."

"Do not be afraid."

"We bring peace."

Wisps of light detached from the floating beings, drifting through the darkness.

"What! Who are you?" the Dark Stranger demanded, spinning around. "What is that light? Why can't I see you?"

"We understand your concerns."

"Please, trust our nature."

"It is the chosen way."

"We are here for you... and the boys."

"The boys?" The Dark Stranger experienced a compelling connection to the light beings, yet his guard remained. "Show yourselves... now!"

Glowing silhouettes thickened in the dark night.

"What are you? Wait... I have seen you—" The Dark Stranger unearthed glimpses of what he assumed were dead, buried thoughts.

"We are from the land of Naculea."

"We bear a mission to bring peace."

"We have been with you before."

He faintly recalled previous interactions with the light beings. Images of the incident with the boys crept into his mind.

"You will remember. It is inside of you."

"You are empowered with the gift."

Taken aback, the Dark Stranger understood what the Naculeans were trying to convey.

"When the boys came upon us, we had to act."

"They are the only hope."

"Druth is near."

"He must be stopped!"

"What! Druth?" the Dark Stranger shouted. "No!"

"We had to act. It was the only way!"

The Dark Stranger's heart ached for the boys. "But they are so young."

"Yet capable... as are you."

"We must protect the people."

"And the nectar."

The Dark Stranger squinted in confusion. "What nectar?"

"The life-source of Naculea." A being's center lit up in waves. "It is here, in the preserve."

"We must have the nectar to live, to empower others to ensure peace. For us and the people."

"The nectar gives power. It is life. Yet if misused, it will cause great destruction."

"Druth must be stopped."

"You must guide the boys."

"It is the only way!"

The Dark Stranger reflected on his own transformation over the last twenty years. It made him distrustful of the Naculeans. "I am slow to accept your reasoning." He turned away from the light beings. "Many changes have come about because of 'this nectar', and you're telling me—"

The light beings disappeared as fast as they had appeared, leading him to believe their guidance was not negotiable.

A single flicker of light passed from his sight.

Frustration had forced tension to the surface in the middle of this lush domain, where the Dark Stranger stood surrounded by a twisted riddle in desperate need of resolution, and in short order.

*With his senses welling, Druth stared at the boys, overhearing them call each other by name. Tingling sensations swirled across his body, causing him to notice something dark, then light.*

# Eighteen
## *Two Gifts*

**W**ITH UNWAVERING DEVOTION to his twisted mission, Druth set out for Danville Heights. With his realistic dreams giving fuel to the fire, he snuck around to get eyes on whoever possessed what he wanted for himself.

Burning urges made him drunk with power. *I am 'the one'. I'm going to take my rightful place. Dreams don't lie!*

Now even stronger was his urge to have all of the gifts, meaning eliminating two of the boys for their senses of smell and taste... if he could find them.

Imbued with powerful senses and instincts, Druth knew how to keep his cool while being crafty. By his estimation, only two more of the gifts were needed for him to become all-powerful. And so, he plotted a course that would ensure his kingdom.

ॐ

Alex used a mechanical pencil and a ruler to bring an idea to life. *An executive office overlooking a river. Perfect! This is one of my best designs.* He slid the instruments across the page, adding opposite corners to enclose a room.

He turned the pages of a well-known book— 'Architecture for the Ages'—his trusted resource for creative thinking. *Let's not forget the rooftop lounge.* He picked up a photography magazine to elicit more ideas. *A living wall? Cool. Painted benches. Wine barrels for mini-gardens. Why not?*

He ripped a page from his sketchbook and tacked it onto a large tri-folded inspiration board. "Josie will love this." He grabbed his phone, tapping his finger onto her picture in his favorites list.

"Hey, I was just about to call you," Josie said.

"Yeah, sorry for not calling sooner." Alex rummaged through items in a drawer, each type of material in its own box. "How's it going?"

Josie sprawled across her bed. "Good. We're getting ready for dinner."

"Oh, okay. Well, I'm working on a 3-D inspiration board. I want you to see it."

"Really? It sounds interesting."

Alex grabbed a few dried cattails and held them to the board. "Yeah, this design is different. It's an office building near the river, so it has a natural feel. Even the rooftop."

Josie ran her fingers through the fringe on an accent pillow. "So, how will you design the board?"

"The major structural elements will go on first. I'll add some magazine cut-outs, then the natural stuff I've been collecting."

"Is that what all those rocks and twigs are for?"

"Yup. And leaves, gravel, bits of wood."

Josie caught on. "You could use foil for the railings to look like steel."

"Oh, cool," Alex said. "See, we make a great team."

"We do." Josie strolled to the kitchen. "By the way, I love the idea of the design firm. Let's talk about it some more."

"Yeah, for sure." Alex glanced at the clock. "I'm heading over to Chase's for a little while. I'll text you goodnight."

"Okay, babe."

"Bye."

Alex beamed at the inspiration board, his cheeks rising. He packed up his tools and set off, his eyes narrowing on his way to Chase's house.

§

*Whack!*

A pool stick slid through Alex's fingers, shoving against the cue ball, which smacked into a rainbow triangle waiting at the other end. A furious scattering of balls placed the guys in limbo.

Alex jumped up and down. "A solid in this pocket right here. Come on!"

124

Rhee preferred to upset the game. "Watch out, I'm looking for a scratch," he said, blowing hard on the cue ball.

Chase watched from the sidelines, champing at the bit. "I'm playing the winner!" It was two out of three, so he would have to wait his turn.

"I'm a senior," Alex reminded Chase, eyeing him from head to toe. "I don't lose to juniors. Okay?"

Chase waved his hand in Alex's face. "Please!"

A solid yellow ball cruised, landing in a side pocket.

"My turn," Rhee said, sinking a blue one with stripes.

"Watch, I'll beat no-playing Rhee, you'll get winner," Alex said, twirling the pool stick, "then I'll take you to school."

Rhee's impatience with the smack-talk had reached its peak. "Okay, you got solids, Alex. Just shoot, man!"

Alex laid into one of his secret angling tricks. "As you wish."

*Smack!*

ॐ

In Danville Heights, a curtain-less window provoked nothing really, unless someone with foul intentions saw it differently. Standing right in front of Chase's window, Druth watched the pool game as his body chemistry shifted in the cool night.

With his senses welling, he stared at the boys, overhearing them call each other by name. *Alex, Rhee.*

Tingling sensations swirled across his body, causing him to notice something dark, then light. *Brown hair, blond hair. I see you!*

Druth saw Alex's tongue mingle with his lips almost the entire time. A bit of the chalk made its way into his mouth.

An air freshener dispensed a spray of fragrance into the room. "Roses, lavender... berries." Rhee sniffed, dissecting the scents.

"Jackpot!" Wicked pleasure washed across Druth as light bounced against the glass.

Headlights cut through the darkness.

Druth ran to evade exposure.

Homebound, Diane gripped the steering wheel as Druth scurried, but not quickly enough. "Hey!" She shouted after him, scrambling for the gear shift, finally clicking it into place.

"Was that your sister?" Rhee asked, looking out the window.

The guys ran outside to see Diane's car idling at an angle in the driveway.

Chase cracked his knuckles. "What's the matter?"

Diane pointed north, her hand tremoring in the trail of the trespasser. "I thought I saw someone looking through our window."

The friends spread out, aiming to catch the offender. But Druth was already speeding back to Sandry Lake to groom Omar and the hooligans to do his dirty work, reaching a new milestone in his quest to be king.

๑

"The taller one has blond hair. The shorter one has dark hair and olive skin." Druth spoke right into the faces of Omar and the thugs. "I'm telling you, they can't be missed."

Omar rubbed his hands together. "What do you want us to do, boss?" he said, palming his knuckles.

Druth flashed one-hundred-dollar bills. "First, take this." He watched the thugs' eyes grow wide.

"We get the picture," Omar said coldly, pocketing the cash, huddling with the others to plan an assault on the two teenage friends.

And in the sky, the yellow moon saw it all, registering the callousness of Druth and his gang of weak-minded followers, trapped beneath the fear of going nowhere without their sad, chosen leader.

*Yet curiously, the little fluttering light ball, having dimmed itself, hiding from Sandy during the exchange between her and Russell, flew from her car.*

## Nineteen

## *Chit, Chit, Chatter*

A SNAZZY RINGTONE alerted Sandy to Russell's call. Already in her car having just finished her shift at the bank, she swiped the screen. "Hey, Russell, how's it going?"

"Well, let's see. I'm almost out of here," Russell said with an easy laugh, "so everything's good with me."

"Hey, I can relate." Sandy organized her purse as the chatter got underway.

"Listen, I won't keep you." Russell stacked papers on his desk before leaving work. "I was at the office last Saturday and didn't see Jordan when he got home. Mason said Jordan was really sleepy, right in the middle of the afternoon."

"Oh, I see," Sandy said.

"He was at your house, right?"

"Well, Jordan wasn't the only one." Sandy put her purse aside. "It was all of them."

"Oh, really?" Russell said, switching the receiver to the other ear. "Did you see anything unusual?"

"They slept until noon, but it seemed like they didn't get enough sleep. I guess they were up all night or something."

"It could have been the excitement of the game."

"I checked the studio but didn't see anything out of order. That doesn't mean I don't have my eyes open, you know."

Russell leaned back in his chair and stared out the window. "Yeah, I hear you."

"I tell you, they were out of it. Really tired, but a different kind of tired. Kinsu practically rubbed his eyes right out of his head. And Alex was so... thirsty."

"I wonder if Jordan was 'thirsty', too," Russell said.

Sandy paused for a moment. "What do you mean?"

"A beer here, a cocktail there. It adds up over time. I would hate for Jordan to end up like Talia." Russell's eyebrows drew inward. "She never envisioned herself as a drinker, but look at what happened to her."

Sandy's cheeks fell flat. "I'm so sorry about Talia."

"Thanks, Sandy. You know, it started innocently, hanging out after production meetings, but that turned into boozing with her friends, from what I could see. I still think about it a lot."

"Seems it was hard for Talia to explain herself. Alcohol is so elusive. It creeps up on you until it's too late. Rhee and I have spoken about it numerous times."

"I tried to intervene, but found myself contemplating divorce," Russell said. "I was so mad, just heartbroken. I didn't want to do it, but I needed to get the boys away from her. And then she died."

"Well, rest assured. I didn't find any alcohol in the studio," Sandy said.

"Interesting. Okay, if anything else comes up, please get in touch and I'll do the same. Otherwise, do you and Rhee need anything?"

"Oh, no thanks. We're doing fine."

"How's work?"

"Good. I'm thinking about going for a management position at the bank."

"That's great. How's the competition?"

"Not too bad, just two other applicants."

"You should put in for it."

"Thanks, Russell, I think I will. Let's stay in touch."

"Okay, take care." Russell placed the receiver onto the phone base on his desk.

Sandy wasn't surprised someone else had noticed how tired the boys had been. She recalled being up all night at that age, too. But their sluggishness had appeared extreme.

Although she was still suspicious she had a schedule to keep, so with key to the ignition her afternoon journey began.

Yet curiously, the little fluttering light ball, having dimmed itself, hiding from Sandy during the exchange between her and Russell, flew from her car.

It sped off to tell the Naculeans about the boys, and to also tell the one who sees and hears much.

૭

Jordan dangled an assortment of lures, their bellies cool with turquoise and mint, others warm with beet and persimmon. The replicas looked real with silver fins and eyes popping out of their heads, but the sharp hooks hidden beneath their flashy tails gave them away.

"Where's my pole?" Wading through a cabinet, he searched for his fishing gear. "There she is." The line and reel were already set.

He placed some of the lures into a small gray tackle box where the sinkers and bobbers lived. He smashed his hat down onto his big waves and eyed a bucket.

*I hope they're biting today.* He reached into his pocket and pulled out a photo of his mother. "Ready, Mom?"

A bright sun framed the picturesque journey to the river. Birds in song delighted in the day. A spattering of tweets rang through the air, going back and forth high in the trees, each one darting into his ears, inviting him into the ballad.

Jordan pressed his finger against the line. He scooped up the bucket and set out for the river.

*Chowder. Fried fish. Chocolate cake. Mom could really cook.* Each of Jordan's steps unearthed a savory memory. *I miss those huge pans of lasagna.*

Waving at passing cars, he took notice of the streets, which his mother had traveled all her life. *If she knew Danville Heights better than anyone, how could she crash on a familiar road?* Doubt lingered in his mind, all the way to the fishing spot.

Whooshing waves slapped against the dock, the noise swelling in Jordan's head. Pressure in the atmosphere magnified, sending vibrations into his eardrum. He stopped for a moment to process the dramatic sounds.

Using the bucket as a stool, he sat tying on bait along with a sinker and bobber. *C'mon, catch me something.*

He stood, throwing the pole back to two o'clock. Easing the reel, he cast the line quite a distance and was satisfied with the hearty plop on the other end.

Jordan propped his pole. His mind drifted. He remembered hearing a door slam, muffling the sounds of a verbal fight between his parents. *As much as I love them both, I'll admit they had some really bad arguments.*

He recalled his father's demands for his mother to stop drinking. He thought back to the time when his mom had appeared unstable.

He reached into his other pocket, this time pulling out two items: his mother's obituary and an article about her

133

car accident. *All of these pieces that don't line up. What happened, Mom?*

Jordan read the items. A dearth of silence lifted the words from the pages. He slumped to his knees, hoping to hear the reel spin, to at least send ripples into the well of pain dragging him down into a sea of the unknown surrounding his mother's death.

*As they walked, the dark night did nothing more than provide a pathway to the next level of confusion waiting among the swirling winds in the peaceful town of Danville Heights.*

# Twenty
## *Trouble in Danville Heights*

A SLAM OF THE CAR DOOR was all it took for Omar and two thugs to begin their mission of fulfilling Druth's wishes. Loosened by the slam, flecks of the car's paint fell to the ground. And with a revved engine, it was pedal to the metal and off to Danville Heights.

Omar slouched down, steering the car with one hand. "We're looking for a kid with blond hair."

One of the thugs scrunched up his face. "I thought you said he had brown hair."

"That's the other kid, dummy."

"So, is it one or two of them?"

Omar shook his head. "Just shut up and follow me."

After slowly circling the café where Diane worked, the car stopped. Its headlights burned through the darkness, hitting the blinds.

They could see a group of teenagers inside. Their presence clearly caused a disturbance as heads began to turn, staring at them through the window.

Omar drove toward the preserve, out of the view of onlookers. "We'll leave the car here." He caught a glimpse of the forest's striking appeal. Then, he and the thugs walked back to where they had spotted the boys, setting out to do the unthinkable.

⎨⎬

"Are you still munching over there?" Diane asked the boys as she cleared the counter, preparing to close the café.

Chase sat across from Alex and Kinsu, who were shoving down the last of their meals. "We're almost done."

Alex smacked his lips. "This apple pie is the best."

"The smothered fries did it for me." Kinsu used a fat potato to sop-up the last of the cheese sauce. "Chase, is your baseball practice Friday or Saturday?"

"Saturday. And that's *if* all my homework is done, so let's bounce." He waved to Diane as they set out for home. "Thanks, sis. See you later."

Diane turned off the neon sign. "Bye, guys."

Chase rode his bike alongside the guys as they headed down the road. They had just passed the post office when he felt a vibration in his arm. "Hold on, something's up."

Kinsu broke into a 360, spinning like a hamster wheel. "Not seeing anything." His laser vision was poised to react to movement.

"Hang on." Alex moved ahead of his friends, peeking around cars and fences with his tongue protruding. "Let me check this area."

Kinsu saw motion near Alex. "Hey, watch out!"

Omar, thick and muscular, stood aside barking commands at the thugs. "Get him!" Moonlight bounced from his bald head.

"What the—" Alex took punches from the thugs, blood flying from his nose.

Mangled faces, hidden by the deep night, twisted and tightened. Gritted, angular teeth jutted from the thugs' mouths.

Kinsu moved in, kicking and punching. Omar ran off past the last building on the block. Potted flowers swayed in the wind of the commotion.

Chase sped after Omar. "Hey, get back here!" He grabbed the baseball bat strapped to his bike and swung it at Omar.

"Keep pedaling, punk!" With the idea of pounding Chase in a dark, secretive place, Omar ran into the preserve, trying to lure him in.

Chase clutched the bat. With his bike thrown sideways, he started after Omar but saw a light coming from inside the preserve. Loud clicks rang out, scaring the heck out of Omar, who came running out straight into Chase's bat.

*Whack!*

With Omar down, Chase sped away to help Alex and Kinsu. He saw Kinsu fighting with one of the thugs, and the other choking Alex. He ran toward Alex and rammed his bat into the thug's ribs.

*Crack!*

The goon stumbled back, releasing Alex. His eyes, yellow, cat-like, had widened. But he recovered quickly and lunged at Chase.

Kinsu broke away and ran toward the yellow-eyed thug, delivering a powerful, airborne, frontal kick, knocking him onto his back.

"What! How did you learn that?" Chase was amazed at Kinsu's strength and precision, but being distracted, they didn't see the other thug getting away.

Kinsu glanced around. "Where'd he go?"

They both looked at Alex, who was lying there, red-faced and wheezing.

Chase extended his hand to Alex. "Are you okay?"

Alex grabbed Chase's hand and got on his feet, then rubbed his neck, which was pulsating with welts. "I think so."

A screeching car sent dust flying as Omar swung through, picking up the runaway thug. "This ain't over!" His round eyes bulged as he sped back to Sandry Lake.

Kinsu charged toward the vehicle. "Oh, it's over, alright. And don't you ever come back here again!"

Kinsu ran to a nearby building, jumped atop the adjoining fence, and climbed to the roof. "They're heading north!" He pointed toward Sandry Lake.

Chase and Alex looked at each other slowly, both uttering, "The north..."

"Hey, what's going on?" the remaining thug asked, coming to, but still dazed.

"What's going on? I'll show you what's going on!" Chase punched him in the face. "Who are you anyway?"

Kinsu grabbed him by the hair. "What are you doing over here?" His fingers slipped and slid through the thug's shiny hair. "Who are you looking for?"

The thug tried getting to his feet, his cat eyes coming into focus. "Looks like you have something somebody wants."

Alex shoved him back down. "You'd better start talking, dude."

"I ain't saying nothing," the thug said. "You'll find out soon enough."

"Fine... have it your way," Alex said.

He and the others lit into the goon, knocking him out cold.

They threw him over Chase's bike, struggling to hold him up as they rolled through the streets, leaving him on the Danville Heights Police Department doorstep with a tag tied to his finger reading: *smelly garbage.*

Alex surveyed his torn, bloody shirt.

"Seems like they were after you, man." Kinsu saw a button on Alex's shirt dangling by a thread. "Do you know those guys?"

"Of course not! I've never seen them before in my life." Alex dabbed at his neck. "What are you trying to say? I don't know anything about this."

"I'm not trying to say anything. It's just... well... that was crazy!" Kinsu said.

Chase rested his forearm on his head. He closed his eyes, taking it all in. "Alright, let's go home."

As they walked, the dark night did nothing more than provide a pathway to the next level of confusion waiting among the swirling winds in the peaceful town of Danville Heights.

*The boys continued home. Blinking lights faintly decorated the midday sky. Their feet moved solemnly, yet the bonds of brotherhood were still intact against the soothing pulse of the river.*

## Twenty-One
# *Voice of the River*

THE SOOTHING VOICE OF THE RIVER calmed the boys' stress-filled minds after last night's attack. During the afternoon walk home, they finally got a chance to bring the others up to speed.

Chase broke it down to Jordan and Rhee. "We got jumped last night."

"Jumped! Here in Danville?" Jordan pressed his hand against Chase, stopping him in his tracks. "By who?"

"I don't know." Chase clasped his hands around his neck. "But it seemed like they were trying to kill Alex."

"Are you serious?" Jordan turned to Alex, noticing the bruises on his neck.

"What's weird is I got this strange sensation before it happened. My arm started to tingle," Chase explained. "Then... *boom*... it was on! We got one of them before he could choke Alex out. We left him at the PD, but two more drove north."

"You know, ever since that night in the forest weird things have been happening." Jordan sensed the assault was staged by deranged individuals.

Chase squinted his eyes and puckered his lips. "We need to get ready in case they come back."

*We never should have gone to the forest.* With his back to the group, Alex fumed at his own bad decision.

"Chase is right, we need a plan," Jordan said.

From a distance, the Dark Stranger overheard the drama as he stood in the brush. His jaw tightened as he walked away quickly.

The boys continued home. Blinking lights faintly decorated the midday sky. Their feet moved solemnly, yet the bonds of brotherhood were still intact against the soothing pulse of the river.

❧

The Dark Stranger sat in his cottage pondering the brazen attack on the boys. Disturbing thoughts consumed him as light spilled in, seeping through the cracks and crevices of the splintered wood.

Stepping outside, he peered into a light-soaked sky from where the two Naculeans were descending straight toward him. There was nowhere to go, nowhere to hide.

"We warned you about Druth."

"We told you to guide the boys."

"Our purpose is to keep the people safe, yet we cannot do this alone."

"You knew this, and yet you linger!"

144

"You must understand. Mankind is in danger, including you."

The Dark Stranger shielded his eyes from the light. "What do you mean... danger?"

"Druth knows of his ability for destruction. It is something we revealed to him some years ago to slow his pace. But it only accelerated his desire for the gifts."

"He is resistant to reason. He defied our directives."

"His quest for power comes from a dark place—a haunting need for recognition."

"It is clear and visible."

"He can feel the gifts. All of them."

"He will not stop until he is empowered with them."

"He is intentional... strong... focused."

"We now realize we should not have told him of his potential for power."

"It was our mistake."

"So you must understand your place!"

"If he succeeds, the nectar will come alive. *It* will seek *him*, empowering him like no other."

"You see, the five gifts were never intended for only one person."

"Should he be empowered, he will control the senses of all of mankind, causing mass destruction and death, including yours."

"Humanity will not survive his trickery, or his emotional pain, which he does not understand."

"He will misuse the gifts against the people."

"Only those he chooses to spare will survive."

"Surely, you have been warned!"

"You must guide the boys to stop Druth."

"It is the only way."

"It is with you now."

Questions rushed into the Dark Stranger's mind. "But, wait—"

Feathered wisps blended into the night sky.

The Naculeans faded into the darkness.

These new revelations pressed against the Dark Stranger's heart, but with a sharp turn to the north, he breathed in new purpose to accomplish a dreaded mission. His turn in the order of life was upon him, and there was no hiding from the call of the night.

*Officer Johnston read the bold headline sprawled across a yellowed newspaper clipping—'Murder in Danville Heights: First in Over 30 Years'.*

# Twenty-Two
## *Cold Case*

OFFICER JOHNSTON, a seasoned, burly patrol cop, opened a large filing cabinet and pulled out a thick folder. Reading glasses rested midway down his nose. The dent between his eyebrows deepened as he perused the contents of the folder, including a photograph of a young man in his late teens with short, curly hair.

He read the bold headline sprawled across a yellowed newspaper clipping—'Murder in Danville Heights: First in Over 30 Years'.

The name of the victim was Ross Dawson.

Johnston had been the first officer on the scene. He remembered it clearly. He had never seen anything like it—a young man bloodied, bruised, and choked to death inside the preserve. He felt deep sorrow for the victim and was still haunted by the traumatic sight.

Shocked bystanders had watched as first responders secured the scene. He recalled pained faces in the crowd whispering and wondering about what had happened.

The coroner's red taillights had showered the bystanders. He remembered seeing Mrs. Perkins's eyes follow the vehicle as it faded from view.

Then, a petite ball of light had gone eye-to-eye with Mrs. Perkins. He saw reflections of light in her pupils. The light ball spewed its dust into her face. She blinked and just stood, watching it float effortlessly toward the heavens.

"Officer Johnston," the records clerk said, a notepad in her hand. "You wanted to see me?"

He looked at the clerk over his glasses, which had slipped a little further down his nose. "Yes, please come in. Have a seat. Just wanted to see if you were able to locate information on Ross Dawson's sports activities, like we discussed."

The clerk sat and thought for a moment. "Sports activities. Yes, I looked into that and found out he wasn't into athletics or on any baseball team."

"He was wearing a baseball cap before he died. He must have lost it. But we recovered it. The hair samples matched." Officer Johnston glanced at Ross's photo in the folder. "People wear caps all the time, but I wondered if there was any special reason he had one on. It's good to go through old files every now and again, just in case we missed something, or someone."

"Is it true, Officer Johnston?" The clerk hugged the notepad. "I mean, what they say about the forest."

Officer Johnston reached over and pushed the filing cabinet drawer, closing it slowly. "You mean the rumors? The gossip? I guess it depends on who said what."

"I've heard a lot about the preserve since I was young. People talked about noises, weird lights, and scary things happening in there." The clerk ran her hand across the back of her neck. "I've never seen any of that myself, nor do I want to."

Officer Johnston looked at the clerk's knee, feeling the tremors of her bouncing it up and down. "Anything can happen to anyone at any time. It's probably best to stay out of there."

"Agreed," she said. "Oh, there's one more thing."

"Sure, what's that?" Officer Johnston asked.

She glanced at her notepad. "Parker. Jordan Parker, Russell's son. He came in here last week requesting the police report related to his mother's death. Said he wanted to know if there was any liquor in her car when she died."

"Really?" Officer Johnston squinched his eyes. "That was a long time ago. I wonder what that's all about."

"I'm not sure. He asked for a copy of the report, then he left."

Officer Johnston thought back to the incident. "There was a bottle of water in Talia's car when she died. That was it. The head-on collision was so tragic."

"I can just imagine. Hopefully, he found what he was looking for." The clerk squeezed her pen and leaned forward. "Is there anything else I can help you with?"

"That's all for now. You've been a great help, thank you." He smiled at the clerk as she exited his office, his cheeks deflating as soon as she was out of view.

As his expression faded to nothing, he stared at the file folder, blinking and thinking. Considering what had happened in Danville Heights many years ago, and with the recent dumping of a thug on his doorstep, he knew all things were possible.

*With the deep charcoal sky offering no comfort to anyone involved, a new chapter had emerged, but how it would unfold remained as cloaked in darkness as 'he' himself.*

# Twenty-Three
## *Out at Night*

COMPARED TO SANDRY LAKE, nightfall in Danville Heights was dreamy. Families gathered in their homes peacefully. Children's eyes fluttered as they winked themselves to sleep. For these were the common routines of the tranquil valley.

There was only one thing out of the ordinary during this particular night—five friends lay awake sensing each other, responding to powerful instincts.

Rhee's nostrils flared, signaling to his friends he was nearby and ready. He took in all the scents of the world.

Each one momentarily experienced visual tension as Kinsu focused his gift.

A salty essence bit their tongues as Alex's heightened sense of taste emerged.

Chase's sensitive hands tensed and flexed, his knuckles protruding then disappearing.

And a soft chime floated into their ears as Jordan audibly scoured the land.

After the attack on Alex, resting peacefully was not an option. Their respective, dominant senses came together as one, channeling their sharp instincts.

Jordan found himself ruffling through black athletic gear. He got dressed, went downstairs, and slipped outside through the garage side door. Each of the boys followed suit, all dressed in dark sports clothes, three in hoodies.

Akin to an alarm clock from hell, their potent instincts were going off, and coupled with dusk, proved a striking combination for action in the dark night.

The five friends walked past the preserve, fixated on the north, occasionally trading glances as their senses burned.

Jordan could hear an altercation unfolding. Angry voices and the pounding of flesh stood out.

Alex licked his lips. Instinctively, he stuck out his tongue, pulled it back, and stuck it out again, detecting wind shifts in the night.

Kinsu's vision sharpened like a razor's edge, capturing the true height of the towering trees, and cutting through the earth to the path leading north.

Chase stretched his arms. Pushing them up and outward, his fingers spread to detect vibrations in the area.

Rhee hunted for scents along the way, some familiar, some foul. His nose burned, the residue filling his head.

The boys ran like a flash to find last night's attackers who had fled north. They gained incredible speed as allies on this journey, which was now quite a ways from home.

Although unsure of the path before them, they charged straight toward Sandry Lake, surrounded by strange, dark shadows in the deep night.

෨

The Dark Stranger shared instincts similar to the boys', but a connection between them had yet to be made. Still, he sensed them running into Sandry Lake.

Feeling the urgency of the situation, he sprung to his feet, yet remained reserved.

He followed them to a dark, familiar place. His black hood wrapped his face tightly, while his cape-like covering blew in the wind, enhancing his commanding presence.

෨

As the boys tore into Sandry Lake, swirling air encircled a dangling sign that swung left to right in a squeaky, unwelcoming manner. Ironically it read— 'Welcome to Sandry Lake'.

Jordan took view of the thrashed town looming before them. "Wow, look at this."

Underfoot, filthy trash greeted them while broken glass served as a guide, hopefully, to the source of this destruction. Filthy or not, Chase stooped and put his hands on the hard terrain, feeling for human vibrations.

"Someone's going at it." Jordan listened intensely, surveying the area for the altercation. "Let's shut it down."

Rhee detected a goon's scent, pinpointing his exact location. "Straight ahead to the right."

"I see them." Kinsu led the way, laser-focused on his target.

Jordan took in the harsh words spit out by the goon who had smacked a citizen onto the dirt.

"Somebody, help!" the person cried.

The thug grabbed at the man's pocket, ripping his pants to steal his wallet. "Be quiet!"

With his makeshift weapon knocked away, the man had become defenseless. He had fallen onto his back, using his legs as a last, self-protective resort. He had covered his face with his hands.

Now at the scene, Alex rushed the goon, and out of nowhere, began fighting him in a style of martial arts for which he had never been trained. "You want my wallet?"

he screamed, punching the thug, beating him down. "That's what I thought!"

Momentary shock consumed the other four as they watched Alex's new moves.

"Did you see that?" Jordan said.

"That was awesome!" Rhee said.

By focusing their new powers, the boys became serious human weapons the goon could not defeat. But taking down one thug was one thing. Three more came out of the shadows with sharp, spiked weapons.

The brewing battle took a turn.

The boys synchronized to outsmart and whip the hooligans as the scared citizen scurried away with his face still covered.

"Alright, get ready," Kinsu said. "Stay close!"

"Look for the ones who attacked us," Chase said.

Alex couldn't tell the difference. "They all look alike."

Chase cracked his knuckles. "Then get 'em all!"

A furious fight ensued with three-on-one, one-on-two, and all in between. The boys dodged the dangerous spikes hurled at them by a vicious band of cruelty used to roaming in dark places, causing mayhem at will.

Chase got hold of one of the weapons, and swinging like a star batter, used it to knock another weapon right out of a goon's hands. He flung both weapons far away.

Mean and muscular, the ruffians fought back with precision, punching and jabbing into eternity. But the boys unleashed their newfound martial arts mastery, and their detailed, accurate moves dazzled beneath the moonlight.

"Two more, left!" Chase yelled, as a pair of thugs joined the fracas.

Their uninvited presence agitated the boys.

"We've got this." Jordan swung and kicked away. "Keep it up!"

The Dark Stranger witnessed it all, yet remained still, allowing the boys to handle themselves as the night wind moved in and out of his black hood. He saw Sandry Lake's dilapidation, which was center stage under the yellow-gray moonlight. *Abandoned homes, streets ripped in every direction,* he thought.

The faithful citizens' last rays of hope had been torn to shreds. He felt a moment of sorrow for this once beautiful township.

As the wind blew, an internal vibration, like a body chill, overcame the Dark Stranger, who was caught off guard by the sensation—a first in over two decades.

He inhaled a volume of air equivalent to the Earth, hoping to identify the source of the essence, clearly linked to someone in the midst. *I think the Naculeans are right!*

The boys kept at it. Their tangle with the ruffians gave new perspective to their potential. They ripped into the thugs, knocking them unconscious.

Like a mound of sorry, soggy laundry, the goons were piled high and left for their leader, whoever that might be hiding in the shadows.

Organized in a guarded, circular fashion, the boys walked toward the creaking, squeaking welcome sign as black crows flew above, causing their senses to flare.

And with the same laser-sharp vision afforded to Kinsu, Druth saw what had happened. "Members of my gang defeated, representative of weakness and a pathetic emptiness?" The boys' prowess struck him and he could not believe his eyes.

Druth stood, concocting a plan to reassemble in order to defend his perch. *Like I said... I will find you!*

With the deep charcoal sky offering no comfort to anyone involved, a new chapter had emerged, but how it would unfold remained as cloaked in darkness as *he* himself.

The school bell would ring in just over seven hours. 'Sleep fast' was an understatement, and unfortunately, there wasn't time to even consider what had just happened.

# Twenty-Four

## *The Encounter*

THE DUAL ROLE of monitoring the boys while keeping watch over vulnerable citizens weighed upon the Dark Stranger. But as always, strength prevailed in the face of adversity. He sprinted away from Sandry Lake, and like many times before, went into the preserve to ponder life's difficulties.

꩜

Now approaching midnight, the hands of the clock indicated there would be no opportunity to turn back under any circumstances.

The school bell would ring in just over seven hours. 'Sleep fast' was an understatement, and unfortunately, there wasn't time to even consider what had just happened.

As the boys returned to Danville Heights, they passed the Dark Stranger's cottage, which was tucked into the woods. They went inside the preserve to catch their breaths and found themselves surrounded by glimmering beauty offering respite from their new challenges.

"In all these years, I've never been to Sandry Lake." Rhee's body tensed with excitement. "That was wild, running over there so fast!"

Bits of light, paired together like peeping eyes, floated amongst faint-blue mist covering the forest floor.

"Seriously! And our senses have changed, too. We can either see, smell, touch, hear, or taste way better than before." Chase examined his hands and arms. "And the fighting... we never did that before. Somehow we're good at it."

Jordan's leg sliced through the air. "Actually, we're great at it. Beating up all those bad guys."

"That night, right here in the preserve, I remember seeing a lot of light," Kinsu recalled, slightly removed from the conversation. "And there was some kind of music, like something I would use for one of my beats."

Chase looked around in the dark. "There's got to be an explanation about what's going on."

Clusters of freckled mushrooms encircled the area.

"It's kind of exciting." Alex pressed against a yawn. "I was mad at those thugs in Sandry Lake, but man, that wore me out. And I've got homework up to here!"

"But we keep going, right?" Jordan asked Alex, taking a peek at his cell phone to check the time. "Don't worry, you'll get your energy back."

"I'm not worried about my energy," Alex said. "I do have homework, you know, and lately, I'm getting questioned by Josie... that's all."

The moonlight angled its way through the forest, cutting across Jordan's face.

"Well... that guy getting beat up for his wallet. Those thugs coming over here. Not happening." Jordan shook his head, trying to make sense of it all. "We're not heroes, but we need to stay alert and stand our ground. And now, we have some kind of powers."

"Yeah, but where did they come from?" Alex asked.

Already inside the preserve, the Dark Stranger heard the boys speaking. He was careful not to alert them to his presence. But as though the universe had convened this moment in time, a sharp wind ripped through the forest, causing the Dark Stranger's cape to flap noisily.

Blinking lights in the midst grew brighter.

Chase's biceps tightened. "What was that?" His eyes darted around, scanning the foliage.

Startled, the boys backed up and got into formation.

Their senses roared as they peered into the preserve at the Dark Stranger's towering outline, expecting to break into hand-to-hand combat at any moment.

Alex spat on the fallen leaves.

Kinsu locked eyes with the Dark Stranger's dramatic profile.

Jordan held his head perfectly still to listen for anyone else who might be hiding.

Chase spread his tingling fingers.

Rhee inhaled deeply, trying to pick up the Dark Stranger's scent.

Although the boys were taken aback, time seemed to be suspended, and the stare-down ensued long and flawlessly. With vein-popping, heart-racing tension full on, clenched fists invited the Dark Stranger to make even one move.

"I'm not going to hurt you," the Dark Stranger said.

Jordan postured boldly. "You're right about that!"

The Dark Stranger raised his hands, assuring them he meant no harm. "I know you've been to Sandry Lake."

Chase glanced at the others. "How do you—"

Headlights glared in the distance, the light cutting through the lush surroundings. Everyone ducked further into the preserve.

"It's Officer Johnston," Kinsu whispered. "He has a flashlight. He's looking around."

The Dark Stranger stood in front of the boys. "Get down."

The five friends marveled at his physical appearance.

*Not seeing any lawless thugs over here.* Officer Johnston walked toward the preserve, the wind's whistle brushing the rim of his hat. "Let's just hope it stays that way."

He jumped into his cruiser and leaned into his radio. "Dispatch. This is Johnston. No signs of trouble or thugs at the preserve. Keep all units out, looking, listening."

He turned the engine, giving the forest a final look. The cruiser's wheels carried him through the streets, ever so slowly.

The Dark Stranger and the boys regrouped.

"Who are you, and how do you know about Sandry Lake?" Jordan demanded, his guard as high as the sky.

The Dark Stranger removed his hood, revealing chiseled features wrapped in an olive tone. "I've been there many times."

Jordan looked puzzled. "You were there when we were there?"

"Yes."

"Why didn't we see you?"

"It wasn't time."

"So, you know about us?"

"I know what happened to you. All of you." The Dark Stranger refused to mince his words. "The poison in Sandry Lake has spread. You must be alert and learn to strike back... together."

"Those thugs in Sandry Lake were in our town. Who are they and what do they want?" Jordan said.

"Those 'thugs' are mere puppets. They follow Druth."

"Who is that?" Jordan asked.

"He's slick. He's their leader, and he's dangerous."

"Seems like they were after us. I mean… Alex."

"I believe it," the Dark Stranger said.

Jordan squinted his eyes. "Yeah, but why?"

"The powers, the gifts inside of you. If he gets the remaining gifts he thinks he needs, terrible things will happen. He'll be in control of the senses of all humans. We must stay focused. It will take all of you, and me, to stop him."

Creases appeared across Chase's face. "This is really getting weird."

"Listen, you cannot defeat him if you separate." The Dark Stranger eyed each of the boys. "You need to stay together. You must stay the course, working as a team."

"We still don't understand how all of this happened." Alex rubbed his eyes, which were red from fatigue. "How did we get these powers in the first place?"

The Dark Stranger sympathized with Alex's waning energy. "You were empowered with the nectar."

"Empowered with what?" Rhee struggled to understand. "A nectar?"

"It seems impossible, but there are light beings among us," the Dark Stranger explained. "They're called Naculeans. They feed on nectar here in the preserve. It's what keeps them alive."

"I knew I saw light." Kinsu stepped into the middle of the group. "It keeps flashing in my mind."

166

Chase recalled Omar having been scared out of his wits. "Yeah, I saw it when that thug ran into the forest."

"Whatever light is inside of them is now inside of you." The Dark Stranger held back the critical detail that he, too, carries the gift.

Jordan lowered his eyes, barely grasping the truth. "So that explains why our senses have changed."

"I will be close by." The Dark Stranger reassured the boys. "It's confusing and hard to understand, but there is a mission to accomplish. Your instincts, and the nectar, will guide you."

Alex yawned again, but listened closely. "Hey, what's your name?" he asked the Dark Stranger, perking up to hear the answer.

The Dark Stranger drew the boys to him. "I'm a… stranger in the dark. Now, watch closely." He demonstrated advanced fighting techniques for their altercations with the thugs.

An undeniable connection soon emerged.

And as the night progressed, the boys learned many things, yet an unanswered 'who was he and from where did he come' remained stubbornly etched into the night.

*A light breeze traveled through the window screen, tossing the curtains. As the boys spoke, little did they know Mason was on the other side of those curtains getting an earful as he helped Della with her window garden plantings.*

# Twenty-Five
## *Game at 4:30*

HOPING THE AUTO CORRECTION feature would help convey his message to Josie, Alex had texted her, letting her know he'd be walking her to school. With only five hours of rest, and some making up to do, an uphill climb loomed.

"Let's see, granola bar. Check. O.J. Check." Alex patted his little brother and sister on their heads and dashed out the door. "Okay, guys, gotta go!"

The door clipped his backpack as it shut.

*School, Josie, chores, and now less sleep. My plate is spilling over.* As gravel danced under his feet, Alex contemplated his life's demands.

Despite the pressure, he thought about his future career and the places throughout the world where modern design influenced the local theme. *When I get a job after college, I'm going to make my mark on the world with my buildings.*

A few steps from Josie's house, a familiar tug—an urge to look north—bit him. But he fought it.

There was only one mission right now: to reassure Josie and get to school. Alex had finally reached her house. His finger met the doorbell. The mood was now up to Josie.

"Well, look who came up for air," Josie said through puckered lips.

Alex braced for the next hit. "I'm sorry about this weekend. I was so tired."

"Oh, really... from what?"

"Well, you know. Hanging with the guys, homework, chores... stuff."

"A text only takes two seconds, Alex." Josie demonstrated her point on her cell phone.

Alex pleaded with puppy dog eyes. "I know. It won't happen again. I promise."

Josie had two choices: blast Alex or let it go. Luckily for him, she held on to the former to use at a later date in case his promise turned out to be empty.

"Alright then, let's go," she said.

Alex grabbed her hand, then glanced toward the north briefly as they made their way to Danville Heights High School.

✇

Della finger tested oven-fresh chocolate chip cookies. "What time are the guys coming by?"

Kinsu had set the stage for the great video game competition. "4:30, Mom."

There would be a fight, or a comedy show, depending on how seriously the warriors got into the game. A chiming doorbell kicked the afternoon into high gear.

"Hey, guys." Kinsu high-fived his four friends, and Mason, who had tagged along with Jordan.

Mason was first in line to get his dessert before dinner. "I love chocolate chip cookies, Miss Della." He stuffed the warm goodness into his mouth.

Della's raised eyebrows humored Mason. "Why, I had no idea." She arranged the last of the cookies on the plate. "Oh, let me see. You love pizza, too, right?"

Mason's eyes grew big. "Pepperoni?"

"Right there in the oven." Della gathered plates and napkins for the impending chow down. "By the way, if you get bored with all this action, you can help me with my plants in the front yard."

"Okay, thanks, Miss Della," Mason said.

With a couple of hours of sunlight remaining, Della went outside to focus on her window garden.

Rhee ripped through the video game with ease. "Hey, watch out!"

"Get back on your side!" Jordan yelled as they battled it out.

Mason salivated at the action on the screen. "When is it going to be my turn?"

Jordan jerked the controls. "Soon, Buddy."

Time passed. Mason kept getting the elbow. *Forget this. I'm going outside to help Miss Della.*

Kinsu peeked around the corner to be sure his mother and Mason were out of sight. After the third game, he made his move. "So, what's our plan?"

"Hopefully, finding those thugs in Sandry Lake and putting an end to all this nonsense," Alex said. "After that, everything should go back to normal."

Kinsu hit the pause button. "The point is... we need an offense right here in Danville Heights."

"Hey! What happened to my avatar?" Rhee checked to be sure his points were still there.

"You all know what I'm talking about," Kinsu said. "The Dark Stranger told us what's going on. Like it or not, we need a plan to deal with this Druth guy and his gang."

"It's already out of control," Alex said, his anxiety creeping in, "and I'm not getting choked again. Okay?"

"We know we can fight, so the plan is simple," Chase said. "Keep going to Sandry Lake until we shut it down. Basically, keep it from coming over here again."

"And how long will that take?" Alex asked.

Jordan glared at Alex. "It doesn't matter, it needs to be done."

"No, it needs to be *organized*. That's the meaning of a plan," Kinsu said, squashing the tension between Jordan and Alex. "Group texting if anything comes up. Traveling in pairs. Meeting at the café if something breaks out. A plan. Roger that, anyone?"

Rhee placed the controller on the couch. "We can all deal with that, but some of our powers are better... I mean... different—"

"What did you say?" Alex got up and stood in front of Rhee.

"Nothing. I said... different. I mean... someone with really strong senses should take the lead, that's all." Rhee leaned sideways and looked to his friends. "You guys know what I meant, right?"

"I know what I heard, Rhee." Alex moved back to the couch, bunching a pillow under his arm.

"Look, those thugs are mean," Kinsu reminded the group, "but we kicked their butts. We can do it again, especially if they come over here."

"Yeah, which might be better because Sandry Lake is a hot mess." Chase recalled the town's filthy streets. "I wonder how it got so bad. I'll pass on the broken glass, you know?"

A light breeze traveled through the window screen, tossing the curtains. As the boys spoke, little did they know Mason was on the other side of those curtains getting an earful as he helped Della with her window garden plantings.

"Hey, how's it going?" Della asked Mason, coming up from behind.

"Super... fine... I mean... great!" Mason was startled to his core, trying to shove his panic down into his soul.

"Wonderful, Mason. I'm so glad you're my helper."

Forcing a smile, Mason was worried about two things: the boys' safety, and Jordan's wrath if he found out he was ear hustling.

He showed Della his good work. "Don't these look nice, Miss Della?" *I'll help Jordan and the guys. I will. I just need some time to think.* Because he was good at figuring things out, he began to brainstorm an action plan.

Della and Mason returned to the kitchen.

"Alright, guys, who's up next?" Kinsu played it off, signaling to his friends they were not alone. "Hey, Mom, thanks for the pizza."

And without a choice, the next in line in the epic video game battle had to grab the controller and get the show back on the road.

*The brothers settled in under dim lights while violent scenes danced in Mason's head until he finally gave in to the zombies on the screen.*

# Twenty-Six
## *Police Matters*

O N THEIR WAY HOME, Jordan and Mason waved at Mrs. Perkins who was admiring the stars on a warm fall night. Back home, things had settled down, which was more than Jordan could have hoped for as the conversation with the guys lingered in his head.

"Hey, Buddy." Jordan kicked off his shoes in the doorway. "How about a scary movie and some popcorn?"

Mason had something specific in mind. "Can I pick the movie?" He wondered how *Zombie Town Part 2* would end.

"Sure thing," Jordan said. "Meet you in ten."

From the moment Mason closed his bedroom door, he counted the minutes, if not the seconds, until the movie was supposed to begin. When Jordan said 'ten', he meant it, so he scrambled to cover at least two bases: changing into his PJs, and calling the police department.

Fear swirled, rushing into his thoughts. *The police need to know what's going on. What will happen to Jordan? Man, I can't believe this!*

Jordan set the microwave to two minutes and turned it on. He went to get the soda out of the fridge, listening for the kernels to pop.

Mason's panic boiled up. *Will the officers investigate? Can they roam around at night to see if there are any fights going on or thugs in the neighborhood? Let me see, what can I tell the police, like… in secret?*

The clock ticked. Mason searched online for the police and safety departments in Danville Heights and Sandry Lake. He scribbled details on yellow stickie notes, shoving one of them inside his pants pocket. *I'd better hurry up. Just a few minutes left.*

Jordan poured drinks for the movie and looked for a popcorn bowl.

Mason dialed the number to the Sandry Lake Security Office. The phone rang endlessly, so he hung up. He hoped for better luck with the second call. But first, he entered a code to block his number.

"Danville Heights Police Department, how may I help you?" the operator said.

"Hello, can I speak to an officer?" Mason whispered, trying not to blow his cover. "I mean, my brother was in a fight. These dangerous guys are after my brother and his friends."

The operator's voice grew concerned. "It sounds like your brother needs to file a police report."

"There were, like, seven or maybe eight guys, and they may be coming back to get my brother."

"What's your name, honey?"

"Ma'am, there was a big fight right here in town!"

"Oh, really? What is your brother's name?"

*What if they think I'm lying?* Mason drifted, remembering the time Dad had told him about Jordan's behavior after his mom's death—acting out and lying constantly because he was hurt and confused. To teach him a lesson, Dad had shown Jordan the overnight jail, Mason remembered his dad saying. He told Jordan his behavior would one day land him in a bad situation. *No telling what Dad will do. Oh, boy, if Jordan finds out I'm calling the police... I'm dead!*

*Ding!*

The microwave sounded.

"Excuse me... are you there?" the operator asked.

Jordan called from downstairs. "Ready, Buddy?"

Mason smothered the receiver. "I'm coming!"

"Can you ask your brother to come to our office to tell us what happened?" the operator asked.

Mason eyed the clock. "No, do you… do you have anyone that can patrol at night?"

"Well, we already do that. Where do you live?"

Mason heard footsteps, wedging him between politeness and discovery. He hung up the call quickly, sticking the phone under the dictionary.

Jordan turned the doorknob to Mason's room and peeked inside. "Time for the movie."

Mason's heart sank as his plan crashed and burned. "Oh, okay. I'm ready." He grabbed his pillow and wiped sweat beads from his forehead on the way downstairs.

The brothers settled in under dim lights while violent scenes danced in Mason's head until he finally gave in to the zombies on the screen.

In the ensuing days, Mason scribbled notes for the cops. Tears stained some of the yellow stickies, which made their way onto patrol cars to get the attention of someone—anyone—who could help.

§

With laundry being the least glamorous of his chores, Jordan grudgingly sorted socks, underwear, and pants so he could get on to other things.

Reaching into pockets, checking for coins and crumpled up dollars, he dug into Mason's pants and discovered a small, yellow wad of paper. He unfolded the stickie. "You've got to be kidding me!"

Mason's pants slid from Jordan's fingers.

The note's contents were clear—'Thugs in Danville Heights. My brother and his friends found them, beat them up far away from home, and left them on a dirty street. Please help before it gets worse!'

The note shook between Jordan's fingers. *Where did Mason get this? Who told him these things?* He marched outside and found Mason playing with his friends, digging for worms in the dirt. "Mason, come here now!" His face grew a deeper red with each passing moment.

Mason glanced between Jordan and the worm he had dropped from the jolt. "What's the matter?"

Jordan gripped Mason, shoving him inside the back door. "Where did you get this?"

Mason found himself eye-to-eye with a crumpled yellow stickie, too scared to speak, but knowing he'd better open his mouth. "Nowhere..."

"What do you mean 'nowhere'? It had to come from somewhere," Jordan said. "Did you write this, Mason?"

Trapped in the hottest frying pan on Earth, Mason had no alternative but to come clean. "Yes, I'm sorry." He dabbed at the sweat on his temples.

"Who told you this stuff?"

"I heard you guys talking at Kinsu's house."

"What! Now, you listen to me." Jordan balled his fist around the note. "The last thing we need is to get in trouble for being out of the house at night."

"I know, Jordan. I wasn't trying to get you in trouble with Dad, but I had to leave those notes for the police because I thought you were in danger!"

Jordan glared as Mason spilled it all. "You did what!" His fist punched a small crater into the wall, narrowly missing Mason's head. "You told the police?"

"No, I had to leave the notes in case they didn't believe me. They don't know who it is. I swear... I never gave them my name!" Mason cried, tearing out the back door.

Jordan snatched at his brother. "Mason, come back here!"

"I'm never coming back!"

Jordan took off after Mason. "It's getting dark. Get back here right now!"

"Get away from me!"

"Mason, I'm sorry for yelling at you."

Mason slowed down, then slumped in a patch of grass, burying his face in his hands.

"Aww, come here, Buddy." Jordan hugged Mason, trying to squash the drama. A lump settled in his throat. *I'll have to tell the guys... straight-up.*

Mason cried into Jordan's lap as the late afternoon sun blanketed the brothers in their moment of pain.

❧

Later that night, Jordan's text to the guys was plain and direct—'gear up and get ready, we have an issue'. Bypassing a pile of homework, he sped off to the preserve.

"What's up, dude?" Kinsu asked. "What was that message about?"

"Mason found out about our powers and the fights." Jordan had no choice but to lay it on the guys. "He's been leaving notes for the cops."

"Why did you tell him?" Chase said, accusing Jordan of the breach.

"What? You know I wouldn't do that," Jordan said. "He heard us talking at Kinsu's."

Rhee's hand covered his eyes. "Oh, great."

"One more thing to deal with," Alex said. "I swear... whenever we go over to Sandry Lake it gets more violent. And now this!"

Jordan assured his friends he would shut Mason down and keep a lid on things. "Don't worry, I got this."

From his dwelling, the Dark Stranger's eyes fixed on the boys as they sped into Sandry Lake, tired, agitated, and wondering if their secret was in jeopardy.

He tore out of his cottage.

"Hey, wait a minute!" He ran close behind the boys, then cut in front of them to slow them down. "Why are you going to Sandry Lake?"

Dust swirled as the boys stopped running.

"To get those thugs," Jordan said.

The Dark Stranger placed his hand on Jordan's shoulder. "You mean to get to the *source* of those thugs, right?" He looked at each of the boys. "Remember our conversation?"

"Seems like we only get so far before we're confronted," Alex said. "We fight back, but we're not really getting anywhere."

"You have two objectives." The Dark Stranger held out his left hand. "First, over here, you need to align your powers like you are one person. As I told you, you must work together." He held out his right hand. "Second, your ground strategy is here. Command it. Be sure the roads are clear, set traps, know the layout. When you enter the town, go in a different way each time. The thugs are blocking you from Druth. Get around them. You'll get a little closer each time."

"It's dark over there, like... there's no electricity, but I can still see clearly, and the moonlight helps." Kinsu shoved a pair of earbuds further into his pocket. "I remember seeing some buildings close to the river. We should check those out, too."

"His gang will come on strong. We'll have to fight our way to the bottom of this," Chase said.

"All of you have the skills, but you must think strategically. Let's go together. Kinsu, you and I will use the rooftops to navigate. You boys, follow along, but spread out." He swung his cape and started to run. "Stay close!"

Swinging into action, the group sped to Sandry Lake with new purpose and new ideas on how to eliminate a great source of frustration threatening the very existence of mankind.

*The child on the right felt sad about his blocks. The child on the left moved further away. Mommy threw rose petals above their heads, yet they singed in the toxic air as they floated and fell.*

# Twenty-Seven
## *Twisted Memories*

**D**RAPED IN DARK COLORS, the child on the left stood far from the child on the right wearing fresh pastels. But pretty toys lured them both. Drawing them together, the play objects brought joy, yet the child on the left had a tear in his eye.

Yearning for his mother to wipe the tear, the child called out but was met only with silence.

Building blocks towered above the child on the right, his proud expression beaming. Yet the thrust of the other child's finger destroyed the delight, and the blocks crashed to the floor.

Mommy appeared, loving both for their good deeds, hugging the children. But the child on the left still felt left out, and his image blurred.

The child on the right felt sad about his blocks. The child on the left moved further away. Mommy threw rose petals above their heads, yet they singed in the toxic air as they floated and fell.

And the sweat that had covered Druth reappeared, and he woke up panting.

"One, two, three, four... five. Five gifts. All mine. All-powerful. Man will fall at my feet!" Druth used a t-shirt to dab his glistening forehead. "The Naculeans speak the truth. The nectar is life."

Moonlight illuminated his tense face.

*There never seemed to be enough love left over. But there are ways to handle that.* Druth wiped mist from his eyes. "It doesn't matter if I was a difficult child. I'm a man now. When the gifts adore me, love will follow."

Searching for objects, he sat on the floor to recreate the dream. The part he could control—building up, knocking down—pleased him. Symbolic of his frustration, he stacked blocks in the middle of the night.

"People are the problem. Only those essential to my desires will survive. There won't be any siblings getting all the love. If I dare be displeased, people will disappear." Druth fumed at the twisted thoughts, but a knock on the door gave his anger a reprieve.

Omar pressed his ear against the door. "Boss?"

"What is it?" Druth snapped, sweeping the objects with his foot.

"I keep hearing noises. Everything okay?"

"Is there no privacy in the world?"

"Just checking on things."

Druth opened the door. "I could sleep more soundly if I wasn't always thinking about how you guys keep screwing things up."

"Like—"

"Like those boys. I said get rid of them. Simple instructions. Were they followed? No!"

"Well—"

"Well, nothing! Hey, if you're not up to the job, just say so. Trust me... I can make other arrangements."

As Druth walked away, Omar saw spilled objects in a corner of the room, and in secret, cast his own evil eye on the evil Druth.

*Alex would need to dig deep to balance his loyalty to the group, and at the same time, deal with the blue hue hanging over Josie's head.*

# Twenty-Eight
## *Blue Girlfriend*

"I WONDER IF THE STARS are this bright on the east coast." Josie sat on Alex's porch, kissing him under the moonlight. "I bet there are so many people scattered all over, just like ants."

"I'm sure the stars are bright." Alex searched his heart for the right response. "But your eyes are brighter."

Josie repositioned herself, snuggling closer to Alex. "One of these days, we'll probably be in a real big city."

Alex glanced to the north. "Yeah, probably."

"Four years of college will be tough, but worth it in the end. We'll need good jobs just to make it." Josie dug in a little deeper. "How are your sketches coming along?"

Alex fought a bitter taste on his tongue. "Fine."

"Hey, what's the matter?"

"Nothing. It's just that everything's been so hectic lately, and I have so many assignments." Alex's eyes drifted. "The guys and I are really tired."

190

"The guys... the games... the homework. I thought we were talking about our future." Josie stood, her cheeks warm. "I wonder what happened to that conversation."

"We are talking about that," Alex said.

"Well, I've applied to three colleges on the east coast, all with design programs. My grades are good enough, so I'm waiting to hear back."

Alex jolted back to the original exchange. "The east coast?"

"We already talked about leaving Danville Heights after high school. It's important to explore options now so we don't get left behind. These colleges are just a few I'm considering. You already knew that."

"Well, I guess you're right, but I didn't know you actually applied."

"Would you prefer I sit here and do nothing?"

"No, I didn't say that."

"I know. You didn't say much of anything except you and 'the guys' were busy."

"That doesn't mean I'm not thinking of you. I mean... of us."

"Oh, with the precious little time you have left for 'us'... that's nice, Alex."

"Why are you mad?"

"I'm not mad."

"You sure sound mad."

"We're supposed to be thinking about the future, but it's hard to do that when you don't even answer your phone half the time!"

Speeding off to Sandry Lake almost every night. Mountains of homework. A constant need to taste everything. Life was happening so fast Alex could hardly make sense of it. Not to mention fatigue as his life's central theme.

Alex slid his fingers into his pocket, then pulled out a yellow ball wrapped in plastic. He squeezed the ball through the crinkled wrapping, and across his lips.

Josie's eyes went from his pocket to his fingers to his mouth. "Sour lemon candy?"

Alex shrugged. A sea of saliva rushed across his tongue.

Josie's frustration had boiled to the surface, but the timing was horrible. "You hate sour candy, or did you forget that, too?"

Alex would need to dig deep to balance his loyalty to the group, and at the same time, deal with the blue hue hanging over Josie's head.

*As Rhee turned into the driveway, the headlights, which he had forgotten to dim a second time, swept across his mom's window. And within moments, a soft light from within her bedroom had appeared.*

# Twenty-Nine
## *The Coveted Gift*

CHASE, THE CURRENT CHAMPION of the video game battle, proudly proclaimed victory. "See, that's how it's done!" He and Rhee had made a bet, and the loser was stuck cleaning Rhee's studio. "Better get to sweeping, dude."

Rhee gathered crumpled snack bags and empty water bottles. "I'll admit it. You took it home, Chase."

"Well, it's about time," Chase said. "My record's been terrible thanks to Jordan."

"Yeah, I know the feeling." Rhee peeped through the window, noticing the light in the kitchen had been turned off. "Looks like my mom went to bed. Let's keep playing. Just keep it down."

Two hours later, they were still gaming.

"Yes! I made it to the third level." Chase stood on the couch, pumping his fist in the air. "I can't believe my luck."

"I don't know about you, but I'm worn out," Rhee said. "Don't we have a test in Mr. —" He looked up to see Chase with his arms spread out, looking through the window.

The squeak of the backyard gate filled their ears.

Rhee picked up a scent. "It smells like Sandry Lake."

Near the cracked studio door, a tiny flicker of light on metal caught the corner of Chase's eye. "Someone's out—"

The door burst open, thrusting a gust of air into Rhee's face. Weathered lines deepened on an angry face. Worn fingers clutched a butcher-blade.

"Where you going, blondie?" a thug said. His stomps shook the ground, the vibrations shooting toward Rhee.

Chase flew from the couch, running over to help his friend. "Rhee!"

The thug cornered Rhee, trying to slash him.

Rhee snapped his neck to the left, dodging the knife.

Chase lit into the thug from behind.

The thug kicked Chase. "Get off me!"

Chase flew sideways. His feet crossed left over right, over and again. A wall-smack to his head dazed him.

Rhee and the hooligan went toe-to-toe. Rhee ducked and body punched him. The thug swung the knife violently. He punched Rhee, knocking him down, and sat on him with the knife to his throat.

Rhee struggled, grabbing the thug's hand, trying to push the knife away as it inched closer to his face.

"It's over for you, blon—" the thug gurgled, clawing at his neck, gasping for air.

Chase, having shook-off the daze, had wrapped his arm around the thug's neck. "No, it's over for you!" he said, pulling the thug off of Rhee while tightening his grip, cutting off the thug's air supply.

Rhee could see the thug fading away. "Chase, that's enough. We got him."

"He was trying to kill you, Rhee." Chase tensed his muscles. "He went straight for you with that knife."

A low gurgle escaped from the thug's mouth.

"I know, but we're not killers." Rhee tried to separate Chase's arm from the thug's neck. "That's enough!" He dug into Chase's bicep, but to no avail.

Mist filled Chase's eyes as his chest rose and fell. "The Dark Stranger's words are coming true. First Alex, and now you. Druth wants the gifts!" He finally loosened his grip on the unconscious hooligan.

A long puff of air escaped from Rhee's mouth. "Let's get him out of here." He surveyed the thrashed room.

"With what? I don't have my bike," Chase said. "Look at him. He's too big for that anyway."

They examined the thug, his pants the color of soot, his hair matted together in greasy clumps.

"We'll have to use my mom's car." Rhee looked out the window to see the house's dark kitchen interior. "She's sleeping. It's the only way."

"Listen, I'm not getting killed by your mom... okay?"

"You got a better idea, Einstein?"

Rhee snuck into the house and grabbed his mom's car keys. *Please help me God because I'm so dead,* he prayed over himself before tip-toeing back to the studio.

"He's heavy. We'll have to drag him to the car." Chase eyed the knife lying on the floor. "He won't need that anymore."

Rhee grabbed the knife and threw it into the trash can along the way. "I swear, I'd better not ever see his ugly face again." He helped Chase drag the hooligan to his mom's car, then he shoved him into the back seat.

Chase sat beside the thug, ready to beat him down if he came to. "I got him. Just get us to the PD in one piece."

"I would if I could concentrate." Rhee's nervous hands deactivated the auto-headlight switch in the car. "We need to drive out of here, dark and quiet."

They drove through the streets to the station, parked the car, and dragged the thug from the vehicle, delivering him to the Danville Heights Police Department. They tied him up and tagged him: *slop for the hogs.*

"That's it, we're out of here," Rhee said. "I just hope Mom's still asleep."

Chase shook his head at the hooligan. "Let's go."

They made their way back. As Rhee turned into the driveway, the headlights, which he had forgotten to dim a second time, swept across his mom's window.

And within moments, a soft light from within her bedroom had appeared.

"Oh, crap... no way." Rhee ducked down, turning off the engine and the lights. "Get out and run home. Right now, Chase!"

Without needing to be told twice, Chase booked it out of there and didn't look back.

Rhee slid out of the car.

Stretching and yawning, Sandy walked to the window and looked outside.

Rhee's feather-like steps carried him into the house.

Sandy checked the clock. It was 12:46 a.m.

Rhee placed the car keys in the basket.

Sandy opened her bedroom door.

Rhee jumped into bed fully clothed, pulling the covers up to his neck.

Sandy peeped into Rhee's room.

Rhee tried to control his breath.

Sandy went to the bathroom, then back to bed.

And by the skin of his teeth, Rhee had escaped his mother's wrath. He lay in bed, shaken, traumatized by the attempt on his life. He realized a new dimension of urgency, and that he was coveted for his gift so desperately sought by the evil Druth.

*Regretfully, this new layer of secrecy had forced Jordan and Mason to define each new day. Hopefully, the weight of it all would not cause further ripping of the already stressed, and extremely fragile, brotherly seams.*

# Thirty

## *Anonymous Writer*

JORDAN SIDE-STEPPED crunchy leaves as he tip-toed back home. With the boys' instincts on speed dial, he felt consistent pressure checkered with exhilaration following their spirited adventures in Sandry Lake.

Stepping onto an upside-down fishing bucket, he hurled himself through a window, crept upstairs, and got back into bed.

From the adjacent bedroom, Mason heard it all. Although painful emotions lingered, he understood his brother's mission. *I'm glad Jordan got back safe.*

Mason's eyelids finally grew heavy, and just in time. For the remainder of the night would be needed to calm and heal them both.

Regretfully, this new layer of secrecy had forced the brothers to define each new day. Hopefully, the weight of it all would not cause further ripping of the already stressed, and extremely fragile, brotherly seams.

৯৯

"Hey, guys, get 'em while they're hot." Russell flaunted his pancake mastery. "Just like Grandma used to make, with fluffy centers and crispy edges."

Hot oil worked its magic on the fresh batter.

Mason slid into the kitchen. "Looks good, Dad."

Jordan followed close behind. "Thanks, Dad."

"Hungry tigers," Russell laughed, observing his sons' abilities to scarf a good meal.

The boys ate, wolfing down the golden pancakes.

Mason looked at his brother. "Uh, Jordan, are you and the guys—"

Jordan gave Mason 'the eye', reminding him not to trip up in front of Dad. "You okay, Bud?" he asked. "Are you full?"

Mason grabbed an apple for his backpack. "Uh-huh."

He went upstairs to grab his things, including a pack of yellow post-its. *Jordan already knows, so a few more notes won't hurt. Anyway, the cops need to hurry up.*

Mason scribbled away.

'If you don't stop them, they will come for you, too.'

'Fighting and danger at night in Sandry Lake!'

'Thugs are coming into Danville Heights. Please catch them!'

After school that day, Mason rode his bike feverishly. Like a newspaper delivery boy, he scoped his targets, and left notes for the cops.

❧

Diane replenished the coffee filters for the evening shift. "We have three rows of new coffee mugs all ready to go," she told her co-worker. "There are plenty of napkins, forks... spoons. You're all set. I'm heading out. See you tomorrow."

She swung her keys all the way to her car. Her fingers slid across the vehicle's smooth, tan interior. She gathered most of her curly hair into a bun. Loose ringlets framed her face as she drove away.

She waved to residents enjoying the fair weather. "Hey, there!" A stop sign provided a moment for her to check her lipstick. A breeze swept through her car, as spinning wheels tickled her peripheral vision.

She turned and looked through the passenger-side window. "Hey, Mason, how was school?"

Mason bit his lip and rode in another direction.

She could see him riding, looking at vehicles. "Well, alright then." She circled a few blocks to see what he was up to.

Mason had pedaled to Billiards Park. His bike lay twisted, the spokes whirling. His body slumped against a tree.

Diane saw him and pulled her car off the road. She found Mason looking down, pools of water in his eyes. She noticed the edge of a pack of yellow stickies protruding from his pocket.

"I'm fine," Mason mumbled as she approached him. He shoved the stickies down into his pocket.

She touched his shoulder. "If you're 'fine', then why are you crying?"

His head swiveled, meeting an oak's trunk. "I'm just tired." He dug his fingers into the tree's grooves.

"You were riding your bike pretty fast to be so tired," she said. "You can talk to me, you know."

Mason leaned his head against the tree, snuggling into the oak. Diane held his hand. Both sat, listening to the patter of leaves in the wind.

৯৹

Dusk approached. The winds shifted inside the preserve. A pulse pumped from within the coveted succulent, beating with life.

"The effort is unfocused."

"Destiny must be... respected."

"It is chosen."

"What is true will come to light."

"The nectar must survive."

"We must divide the plant... to live... for peace."

"It is the only way."

The Naculeans urgently discussed their plan to propagate their life-source to spread peace and empower others.

"We must act soon."

"Druth is advancing."

"We may not survive."

The little light ball, which was tucked beneath a sprawling frond, sensed doom among the rising stakes growing more violent each day under the gloomy skies of Sandry Lake.

੧

"I'm telling you, he looked really sad yesterday." Diane wiped the counters with her phone wedged between her shoulder and her ear. "No, I'm still at the café closing up for the night. I'm just about to turn off the sign and lock the door. Chase, you might want to speak to Jordan about Mason."

Chase's face and his fist tensed at the same time. "I will. I'll see him at school tomorrow."

"He's a happy kid. I was surprised to see him cr—"

The café's neon sign pulsed under the night sky. A dark spot swelled on the other side of the blinds.

"Diane? What's wrong?" Chase's voice took on an edge of worry.

A twisting door-knob shoved Diane's heartbeat into her throat. Her shoulder weakened, losing grip on her phone, which slammed to the ground.

"Diane!" Chase yelled.

She glanced toward the coffee pots, napkin holders, mugs—anything to aid her defense.

The door opened. The hanging bell's familiar ding floated up and away. The toe of someone's shoe moved into the entryway. "You're that kid's sister."

Diane could see fingers wrapped around the door's edge. *Oh… my—*

She dashed for the flood lights switch. From under the awning, bright streaks splattered across the glass as she flipped it with the tip of her nail.

The goon had been made. His hand retreated, slamming the door shut. He searched for a crevice in which to hide, but the moonlight had sucked him in, and he ran away.

Diane's lungs collapsed. She buried her chin into her chest. She rushed to secure the door, then staggered across the floor to find her phone. She saw the cracked face of her device.

Minutes had passed. Another shadow appeared. "Who's there?" She dropped her phone again with the bang on the door.

"It's me… open up!" Chase said.

Her trembling fingers fumbled with the lock.

Chase burst in, checking every corner of the eatery. "What happened?"

She looked outside, down the street. "I don't know who that was! But he said, 'You're that kid's sister'. I'm sure I heard that. What did that mean? Are you in some kind of trouble?"

Chase gritted his teeth. "No!"

"Well then, what was that all about?" Diane asked.

"I don't know, but don't worry." Chase squeezed his hands around an invisible baseball bat. "I got you. Nothing's ever gonna happen to you, sis."

*Although he trusted his son, Juson knew at Kinsu's age there were bound to be all sorts of teenage antics feverishly waiting in the wings. He pulled the door, centimeter by centimeter, watching Kinsu until the last second.*

# Thirty-One
## *Out of Character*

THE GARBAGE TRUCK'S grinding wheels cut through the silence. Sandy, taking an early shift at the bank, applied her make-up, slipped into her shoes, and checked the clock. "Time to go."

Backing out of the driveway, she saw a garbage can on the curb at the house next door, but hers was nowhere to be found. *Now who would aspire to be a garbage can thief?*

The garbage truck approached quickly while her can was still sitting inside the back gate. She got out of the car, running to grab her can in time. *This isn't my job. I'll tell you what, we'll have a talk when I get home.*

Sandy began dragging the can to the curb.

The truck's rusty brakes squeaked loudly as Rhee busted through the front door wearing only his underwear. "Mom, I'm sorry!" He grabbed the can from his mom. "I forgot to put it out last night."

Sandy dusted off her skirt and got back in her car. "Get your calendar in order, Rhee!"

His overgrown fingernails scratched through his thrashed hair. Still barefoot, Rhee went back inside, straight toward a long and uncertain day.

ॐ

"Mr. Knowlton's class just keeps getting harder." Jordan eased his chin toward his chest, stretching his neck muscles as he walked home with Rhee. "I swear, I'm going to find the money to pay someone to sit in that class for me."

"Well, it is science." Rhee's finger traced a figure eight. "Let's invent a way for the class to disappear."

"You mean like *poof* into outer space?"

"Yeah, a serious *poof*."

"Man, we could sell it to other high schoolers."

"Now, that's what I'm talking—" Rhee dropped his books. His hands pitched a tent over his nose. "Ouch!"

Jordan searched the area for a threat. "What's the matter?" He heard a rustle in the brush.

Rhee bent down. "A stench... shooting through my... nose." He saw a fluffy tail emerge from the bushes, part of it black, the other white.

Jordan caught the scent, too. "Skunk!"

A breeze carried the creature's odor. It swirled in the air, producing a toxic nasal cocktail too strong for Rhee's acute sense of smell.

"Let's get out of here." Jordan walked with his friend to fresher ground.

"That was painful!" Rhee buried his nose in his elbow. "It usually stinks, but this time it hurt."

"Dude, you should have seen your face," Jordan said.

Rhee shook his head. "Always something..."

Jordan slapped his thigh. "Man, that was worse than the locker room after practice!"

Rhee looked over his shoulder to be sure they were in the clear. "Tell me about it."

The two friends laughed and split up at the corner, heading their separate ways.

୭

Jordan walked into his house to find Russell and Mason sorting bills.

Russell reviewed a credit card statement. "Son, as they say, 'Be sure to marry an accountant.'"

Mason smiled as he munched on tortilla chips. "Hey, Jordan."

Jordan yawned as he headed for the kitchen. "Hey, what's up, Bud? Hi, Dad." He scratched at his ear.

Russell took notice of his son's fatigue.

Jordan grabbed a snack, hit the stairs, and shut his door loudly.

His dad followed him and opened the door. "Is everything alright? The door slammed pretty hard."

"Yeah, I'm doing okay, just tired." Jordan ran his fingers across his ear, then squeezed his earlobe. "I didn't hear the door slam."

"What's wrong with your ear?" Russell asked.

Jordan's hand fell to his lap. "Nothing."

"The door," Russell said. "It shook all the paintings in the house and you didn't hear it slam?"

Jordan's eyebrows squished together. "No."

Russell glanced around the room. "Don't forget those dishes, son. They won't put themselves away."

"Alright." Jordan prepared for yet another task piled atop the stack already staring him in the face.

Russell began to close the door.

"Uh, Dad. There is something. I've been thinking about Mom a lot lately." Jordan tapped a pen against his desk. "We just celebrated her birthday. It gets hard sometimes, you know."

"I know. I think about her every day. She took good care of you and Mason. I know you miss her."

"The car accident. It makes me wonder if her tire blew out, or if she had engine trouble. It seems weird, especially since she knew the roads around here."

"Talia's car was in perfect condition. I saw to that. It bothers me, too, but that couldn't have been it. She had a drinking problem. I've been honest with you boys about her challenges."

"Yeah, we know. It's just that, well... I seem to miss her more when I'm stressed. Lots of homework. Lots going on."

"I feel you. Just know Mom is smiling down on you, and I'm here for you and Mason. We can talk about anything. Okay?

"Okay, Dad."

Russell closed the door and rejoined Mason downstairs.

Jordan reached into his desk drawer and pulled out an album filled with his mother's photos, along with a copy of the police report of her car accident.

He circled the contact details of the other driver—a surviving witness to the crash. He took a deep breath and wrapped his fingers around his phone. "Stay calm." His stomach turned, causing him to hesitate. *Just punch the numbers.*

The seventh digit sealed the deal.

"Hello... May I speak with Mr. Adams... I'm calling about the car accident involving Sidney Adams and Talia Platero. I'm looking for some information."

Jordan's head rested in his hand the entire time. He closed his eyes. The room went dark. A loud gulp caused his eyes to blink.

The voice on the other line was soft and gentle.

"What?" Jordan opened his eyes. "No, I didn't know Mr. Adams had died three months ago... I'm so sorry for your loss, ma'am... Goodbye."

Jordan's head hit the desk. A sick feeling invaded his chest. A moment of truth destroyed. He felt the energy drain from his body, melting into a black hole where answers to his mother's death remained elusive and beyond his reach.

ॐ

Della and Juson enjoyed hot tea under the stars.

"I think it's time we added twin hammocks out here." Della adjusted the cushion under her feet. "What do you think, honey?"

Juson munched on snacks, waiting for his tea to cool down. "Sounds relaxing."

They sat, pondering the simple things in life, but were interrupted by a noise on the other side of the house.

Della jumped to her feet. "I heard something."

"Stay here." Juson guided Della back to her chair. "I'll check it out."

Not seeing anyone, he passed by Kinsu's bedroom, noticing a protruding corner of the window screen. A light breeze caused the curtains to sway.

He went inside to see if Kinsu was in bed. *It's a school night. He had better be in there for his sake.*

Kinsu lay silently under his covers, appearing to be asleep when his dad opened the door. *Oh, crap... I just had to fall sneaking through the window.*

Juson leaned in and looked around, his eyes shifting between Kinsu and the swaying curtains.

Kinsu had just returned from Sandry Lake. Part of the mishap had revealed itself and was still clearly visible.

With his eyes closed, his heart thumping, Kinsu lay still. *Maybe I should snore a little. No, that would be too much. Just lay here. Boy, if I get caught...* Kinsu played the part until his dad left the room.

Although he trusted his son, Juson knew at Kinsu's age there were bound to be all sorts of teenage antics feverishly waiting in the wings. He pulled the door, centimeter by centimeter, watching Kinsu until the last second.

Tension spilled from Kinsu's body as the door lock clinked at last. *This is getting ridiculous. Maybe I should just tell my dad.*

He observed the room, free of light, void of stimuli. A refuge. A place to heal from the onslaught. But now a space threatening to upset his family. *I need to think.*

His line of sight shifted as he moved around, landing on a baseball cap on the floor near his nightstand. *Never thought I'd be wearing a hat this often. But sometimes I need to shield my eyes from the sun. I don't think anyone's noticed. At least I hope not.*

Kinsu reached for the earbuds near his lamp where the bulb had been wrapped with a hand towel to dim the light. *I don't care what happens. Nothing can get in the way of me winning the beat contest. I'm close, but I need to work on my track. I just need more time.*

He tapped his music player and adjusted the buds. *I'm sorry, Dad,* he thought, as the rhythm slapped to the pulse of his heart, sending guilt straight to his soul.

*The slight, tattered woman, with her blonde curls gathered into a high bun, held her little daughter's hand. There was no one else to watch the child, and the pain of hunger had reached a new plateau.*

# Thirty-Two
## *Perfect Conditions*

T HE TICK-TOCK OF THE CLOCK, the dark night, and creaking, cracked boards underfoot paved the way for the boys as they returned to Sandry Lake. Jordan reaffirmed their intention. "There's only one goal here—to stop Druth. The quicker, the better."

The friends observed several ruffians attempting to break into an abandoned boating area. The thugs spewed chatter in the spirit of their leader.

"Let's prove to *him* what we can do." A big, ugly hooligan sloppily chomped on a thick piece of jerky. "Go get that speedboat over there. It's ours now."

Jordan felt the thugs' sinister energy. His muscles began to tense as their ramblings revealed just how low they would go.

Making their way up a dark, damp boat ramp, the boys could see the goons more clearly.

"All this stuff is new. Look at this." A thug admired the boat's accessories. "Get to it. Stack it up!"

"We'll need to take down the big one strategically, so get ready," Jordan said to the others, waiting for the right time to strike.

The wind's howl swept the scene.

The boys tightened their fists.

Chase made the first move, rushing one of the thugs. "You want some of this?" He swept him backward, causing the thug to smash against a hard surface.

Dust and debris covered the scene as Alex moved in swinging a garbage can lid, which hit the thug in the head. "Who's next?"

Chase and Alex slapped their palms together.

Nearby, Jordan sat on top of another thug, repeatedly punching him in the face. When two more witnessed Jordan fracturing the thug's nose, they ran away.

Kinsu raced after them. "I'll get 'em!"

Chase, Alex, and Rhee drew near each other, surveying the scene. Several thugs advanced toward them with weapons in their hands.

Rhee sized up the goons. "Stay close!"

The big one fashioned a sharp weapon out of nearby scrap metal and jute rope. Spit flew from his mouth. The boys charged forward to finish their business in anticipation of getting to the big one.

Their martial arts excellence could not be denied as kicking, punching, and blocking ascended to new levels, with the night growing darker as they struck.

Jordan joined the group. "Hey, where's Kinsu?"

With a choppy exhale and a massive inhale, Rhee located Kinsu's scent. "He's over there," he said, pointing west.

"I'll be back." Jordan ran westward to find his friend.

☙

Although warned not to wander out at night, the remaining citizens of Sandry Lake would sometimes venture to find food or their stolen belongings.

An independent spirit who had made a tiny home for herself and her child looked around cautiously. The slight, tattered woman, with her blonde curls gathered into a high bun, held her little daughter's hand. There was no one else to watch the child, and the pain of hunger had reached a new plateau.

"Come on, baby. Be real quiet. We're going outside for just a few minutes." She closed the door behind them. "Stay with Mama."

She rummaged through boxes stacked outside an abandoned shop, but only found a few cans to carry in her skirt. *Is this shop unlocked? Maybe there's more inside.*

The door opened, but the rusty hinges squeaked loudly, signaling to the two runaway thugs that someone was nearby.

In no time, the goons were upon her. Too scared to move, she could neither barricade the door nor run.

Clutching her child, she screamed at the top of her voice while flinging boxes, cans, and trash at the lawless thugs. "Someone, please help!" She placed the child on the floor to fight harder.

By this time, Jordan had found Kinsu further down the same block. The woman's deafening screams lit up his ears. He spun around.

Kinsu had the commotion within his line of sight and was able to see their faces. "Let's go!"

Taking mere seconds to arrive, Jordan and Kinsu lashed a beating upon the thugs they would never forget. Boxes, trash cans, and other junk flew into the air as the thugs took the beat down.

And as the swirl of commotion unfolded, the woman stood there in a surreal state. It was the first time a citizen had seen the boys. As she snapped back, she searched for her child who was crouched in a corner. "Baby, come to Mama!"

With the thugs sprawled across the floor, a lone canned good rolled between the woman and the boys, drawing everyone's attention to it, then to each other.

Kinsu broke the ice. "Are you okay, miss?"

The woman nodded in silence as her little daughter clutched her curly, blonde bun for dear life.

*The wind howled. Their gaze focused in as they locked eyes. The slow-moving atmosphere lent distinction to the moment—a turning point in the winning of the war against evil.*

# Thirty-Three
## *Seen Yet Unseen*

"**W**HERE ARE YOU?" A stout, panicked man roamed the area. His shirt collar butted up against his wild beard. He searched in the darkness, looking through windows and behind doors.

Jordan heard the man. "We've got company." He turned around, looking out the window. He tapped Kinsu on the arm. "Check it out."

Stepping over trash, the man scanned the buildings. He walked past the window of the abandoned shop, locking eyes with Jordan. He moved in close, initially unsure if this was some kind of reflection.

His furrowed brow crinkled even deeper. "I'm so sick of these thugs!" The man picked up a heavy object to hurl it through the window.

"Wait!" the blonde woman cried, rushing outside with the child still clutching her hair. "They saved me."

Jordan and Kinsu followed her outside.

"There you are. I was worried sick about you," the man said. "Who are they?"

"I don't know. I've never seen them before."

"Did they hurt you?"

"No... I'm just so glad you found me."

The man comforted the woman as she began to cry.

"What's going on over here?" Kinsu asked the man. "Don't you all have any food?"

"Someone has seized our town. It's been pure hell," the man said. "We're fending for ourselves."

Jordan could appreciate the man's compassion for his friend. "We're looking for the source, but we need your help." He pointed toward the edge of town. "What's over there, on those hills?"

"Abandoned homes and shacks," the man said.

"And where do these roads lead?"

"Toward the next town, Lavender Quarry."

Jordan and Kinsu looked at each other. Kinsu turned to see a bridge in the distance.

"It's dark out here. There's only one street light for this whole area?" Jordan asked.

"We had plenty of light. Now it's either shut off or busted out," the woman said, stroking her little daughter's hair.

Kinsu felt their plight. "We're looking for someone named Druth. His gang is everywhere. They're coming into Danville Heights, too. Have you seen him? We're trying to stop him."

The woman sobbed. "No, but bless you. Both of you." She buried her face in her friend's beard.

"Sir, where do you live?" Kinsu asked. "And where's the grocer?"

The man pointed to a nearby row of small, boarded up commercial shops. "We live over there, but there are no more grocers."

Jordan looked toward the hills once more. "Let's tell the others." He eyed Kinsu, then jerked his head to the left.

"What 'others' are you talk—" the man said.

And as fast as they had arrived, Jordan and Kinsu disappeared into the night, leaving no clue as to who they were. With the task completed, they were off to help their friends.

ℱ

"Little boys who think they're tough. I'll show you who's tough!" The big, ugly hooligan swung his sharp weapon at the boys, nearly slicing into Chase in the wild ruckus.

"What's going on?" Jordan arrived on the scene with Kinsu. "C'mon, man, let's jump in there."

The thug growled at their presence, spitting at Jordan's feet. "I'll take you out!"

"Surround him. Keep your eyes on him," Alex said.

The boys stared him down, signaling each other with their eyes, communicating that this would be a double-sided job—some in the front, and some in the back. They split up and went to work navigating the take-down.

Jordan and Kinsu bobbed and weaved, dodging the sharp weapon. "Be careful, Kinsu!" Jordan yelled.

Kinsu landed solid punches on the thug's head, closely missing the jagged scrap metal.

At the same time, Rhee, Chase, and Alex worked the backside with thrashing kicks and punches.

"Where's that rope he was using?" Kinsu scanned the dirty surface for the leftover jute. "Wait, I see it... right there. Grab it!"

Chase ran to get the rope. "Here, Alex, take it. Climb up on my shoulders." He tied knots with precision.

Chase and Alex assembled into a human ladder to tackle the big one. Perched on Chase's shoulders, Alex flung the rope around the hooligan's neck. As they disassembled, Alex swung wildly, choking the hooligan.

Rhee grabbed Alex's ankles, pulling him, tightening the rope's pressure while the others unleashed a painful assault onto the big, beefy thug.

As his knees hit the dirt, ugly grunts filled the air. Slipping into la-la land, the thug's eyes began to flutter.

"That's right, time for bed." Kinsu cradled an invisible infant, rocking his arms. "Let's see... where's your blankie? And listen, if you even think about coming over to Danville Heights... you're dead!"

"Tie him up tight so he can't escape." Jordan tossed the last of the rope to the guys. "Let's move out. One more sweep."

Kinsu thought of the woman and her toddler. "Hopefully, we won't find any more people who shouldn't be out here right now."

Leaving the tied-up thug by the side of the road, the boys formed a tight circle and walked through Sandry Lake looking, listening, and smelling for Druth.

∽

The blonde woman and her bearded friend found their way back to safety. They remained fixated on the young heroes who took down the thugs.

"He said, 'the others'. I hope they're not another round of bandits in disguise," the man said, holding his head, his expression revealing a heavy sorrow.

Tears welled in the woman's eyes. "What should we tell our friends?"

"We'll tell them the truth."

"I don't know how we would handle another attack right now," she said. "We're barely holding on as it is."

The two approached an abandoned garage in which the man lived with his friends. And with a secret, Morse code-like knock, the door opened.

"Listen, everyone, something just happened," the man said, watching the onlookers' expressions as he broke the news.

Candles flickered against pained faces.

As their eyes widened in disbelief, the woman covered her child's ears to block out the recent memory, praying it would fade away into another day.

��

"I think we're good for now." Chase dusted off his ripped jeans. "But we need to flush this evil out before it comes back into Danville Heights."

"Who knows, some of those losers might be over there right now." Jordan examined a deep scratch on his hand. "If we don't get to it, things will get worse."

The boys stood in a grassy area, not far from a row of multi-story tenements. The tall blades swayed to the will of the wind.

Alex checked his phone for the time, noticing a text from Josie. "You heard the Dark Stranger. It's already a lot worse."

As they conversed, their few words floated up and into *his* ear space.

"Shut up!" Druth shushed the goons vying for his attention. He stepped onto the balcony of a two-story building. His senses of sound, sight, and touch burned in the night. "Visitors?" He smacked his chapped lips, scanning the streets below with his powerful vision. "The five friends. Persistent, I tell you."

A ball of light could be seen from afar. Swirling in from above, the little light being observed the scene including the Dark Stranger moving around on a rooftop not far from the boys.

The Dark Stranger's dramatic senses came alive. His telescope-like vision fixed on Druth. *What the...*

Zooming in from the opposite end, Druth stood rigidly. He noticed black fabric moving around in the wind. *What is that?*

While trying to maintain an eye upon the retreating boys who were speeding out of Sandry Lake, Druth began to seethe as his vision sharpened, seeking to clarify the distracting wave in the distance.

Druth's deep breathing struck the Dark Stranger, whose own acute sense of hearing had flared, capturing his movements.

As each of their senses grew stronger and more defined, they recognized the other, which thrust them into a fractured sense of reality. Beyond seeing and hearing, emotions raged, causing each to grapple with what they knew of the other.

The wind howled. Their gaze focused in as they locked eyes. The slow-moving atmosphere lent distinction to the moment—a turning point in the winning of the war against evil.

And as the seething reached its peak, Druth loosened a portion of the balcony's splintered rail and flung it, shattering it into a thousand pieces.

Jordan heard the loud crash all the way in the preserve. "Whoa—"

The light ball jerked, then flew away.

The Dark Stranger saw a cloud of dust rise from the tall grass. *It's him alright.*

Foam spilled from Druth's lips. Stepping into the doorway, his jagged fingernails dug deep into the tattered frame. "You dare to approach me?" he roared in thick echoes, his words setting the tone of his stance. "Come on, come closer!"

Druth's screams ripped through the Dark Stranger, causing pain in his ears. Memories related to this specific tone of voice became vivid. But his guarded pause lasted only seconds. He swung his cape and disappeared into the night.

*The Naculeans were right. As bad as it is, it's now or never*, he thought, as he reached the edge of the preserve.

Desperately panting from the incredible sprint, he knew the first rays of the day of reckoning had arrived, and it was time to embrace the light of a new day.

*Jordan could feel the others sitting upright in their beds having just escaped the same dark dream, which was more real than the boys could have ever imagined.*

# Thirty-Four
## *Protect the Gifts*

PAIN CONSUMED forty thousand people. Unceasing, horrible ringing spilled into their ears, bleeding them to their deaths. Children cried. Black mist covered the land.

Sixty thousand more appeared, but the light of day was too much and their eyes exploded, killing them all.

Weeping swirls of light stood afar growing weak due to a vanishing life-source. Pained clacks showered the land, which crippled the ones with sensitive ears.

A young girl reached out, but no one saw her. Fallen leaves turned into charcoal dust, smothering her last breath.

The king of the land was overjoyed, settled in his soul, prideful of the puppet strings littering his domain.

His men flung food and ate merrily.

Huge leaves withered. Mold spread throughout. For the nectar had soured, the foul perfume killing another eighty thousand.

A whisper rippled in the distance warning, "A part of you is coming for you. Protect your gift!"

And then, a puff of light flew into the faces of the five friends, and they all woke up.

Jordan jumped out of bed, breathing rapidly, fear coursing through his body. "Who's there?" His mother's photo beamed from his bedside table. He grabbed the frame and held it close to his heart, and sat on the edge of his desk chair. *Mom, are you here? I found out you weren't drinking that night. What happened to you? Seems we're all going to die. I'm scared, Mom. I wish you were here.*

He found comfort away from the disturbing dream, which the Naculeans had accurately foreshadowed.

Druth was coming—and if the nectar found him—he would destroy all of humanity through their senses.

Jordan could feel the others sitting upright in their beds having just escaped the same dark dream, which was more real than the boys could have ever imagined.

❧

Morning had arrived. Mrs. Perkins rocked on her porch, gazing at Gerber daisies spilling out of hand-painted pots. A light ball clicked to her. It flew effortlessly, greeting her.

"Hello, little one," she clicked back, taken with its fluttering wings.

The clicks reverberated, traveling down the street to where Mason and Jordan were walking to school.

234

"I hear noise." Mason's head swiveled. "Is that music?"

As they approached Mrs. Perkins's house, Jordan saw her playing with the light ball. "Mrs. Perkins, is everything okay?"

He studied the curious exchange.

"Why, of course, dear," she replied, waving her hand, shooing the light ball. "Are you boys ready for school?"

Jordan answered slowly. "Always... Mrs. Perkins."

She walked down the steps, closer to the boys. "Only good students are 'always' ready for school. Very good. But one more thing." Her voice grew deeper, her eyes pierced into Jordan. "Respect your father... yet honor your destiny. You must draw from within yourself at the right moment in time."

Hairs rose on Jordan's neck. *What! Does she know?* His racing thoughts slammed into the corners of his mind. "Yes... ma'am."

And with his next step, the light ball swooped in, cutting in front of his face, practically lifting the waves in Jordan's hair.

Mrs. Perkins's eyes cast a faint glow. She smiled at the brothers, who were doused with unspoken tension, trying to hold on while invisible walls closed in on them from all sides.

Mason got an eerie feeling. "Let's go, Jordan."

The light ball raced to the sky to find the Naculeans.

The brothers walked to school, glancing over their shoulders most of the way.

༄

A sea of students rode the wave of a packed hallway, straight toward a rectangular cafeteria with long rows of beige benches connected to tables. A 'Chargers Pride' banner hung from the wall.

"Hey, where are you going?" Jordan asked Chase. He sunk his teeth into a burger.

A slice of pizza dangled from Chase's hand. "To see about Diane." He moved past a group of gamers, off to a quiet spot. He sat on the school lawn, which looked like thick stripes of light and dark green carpet.

His thumb scrolled, dialing his sister.

"Is my little brother checking on me?" Diane said. "How thoughtful of you, Chase."

He sat tall. "Well, after the other night, I just want to know you're okay." He nipped at the crust.

"Everything's back to normal. I'm fine," she said. "Mom would be proud of you."

A knot in the pit of Chase's stomach made him pause. "I want to be the man she would want me to be."

"You're young. It takes time, but you will be," Diane said. "Showing concern for others is a big step."

Chase drifted, recalling the time he had seen his mother in the hospital. He had smoothed her hair. "Mom told us to stay tight."

Diane glanced around their home, filled with splashes of their mother's favorite color: red. "Yes, she did, and we are. We have to carry her torch, together."

"Well, I'm glad you're okay," Chase said.

Diane glanced at Chase's childhood photo on the desk, examining the toothless boy in an oversized batter's helmet. "I'm much better now."

஧

Chase and Rhee passed the bike shop on their way home from school.

"I worry about Diane." Chase's heavy backpack slipped down his shoulder a notch and he hiked it back up. "Sometimes she's alone at the café. I'm not sure what she would do if one of those goons actually went in there."

"We'll all keep an eye on her." Rhee flapped his t-shirt, letting his body heat escape. "We should start doing our homework at the café."

They cut across the street, tucking under a row of shade trees on the next block.

"That's where I'm headed," Chase said. "I was going to suggest that to the guys. Want to come?"

"Naw, I'll join you tomorrow," Rhee said. "I told my mom I'd stop by to see her."

"Is she alright? Did anything happen?"

"No, but I'm the man of the house, you know."

"Me, too, or at least I'm supposed to be." Chase shielded the sun's glare. "I need to do better."

"Anyway, you already knew that my dad used drugs. When my mom and I moved from another state when I was three, she was trying to get away from all of that. She's been open about it." Rhee tucked his history book under his arm. "He's alive, but we hardly ever talk. It's on me now."

River rock lined an entryway, framing a market, coffee shop, and bait and tackle store. Oak trees welcomed the pair as they swung left.

"It's hard, I know. My dad hasn't been around since I was little. He was in the military and my mom was a nurse at the base. That's how they met," Chase said. "They split up when he went overseas, and that's pretty much the end of the story." He pointed toward the bank a few streets ahead. "And there she is."

Mason and some of his friends whizzed by on their bikes. He broke away from the group, heading down a side street.

"Where's he going?" Chase asked.

Rhee's near-transparent eyebrows rose. "No telling."

He stepped onto the bank's parking lot, then looked across the street to see tables and chairs lining the curb at the ice cream parlor.

"We're the men in our families and we're only in high school," Chase said. "How crazy is that?"

"I hear you." Rhee watched a colorful flag wave at the ice cream shop. "Alright, bro, see you later."

Their palms smacked. Their shoulders bumped.

As Chase headed toward the café, Rhee walked off, squinting at the asphalt glaring beneath the sun. His family, his whole life traveled the road of his emotions, darting around in the darkness of his troubled mind.

*The complex web of chaos enveloping the two towns, and the continuous interference from all the different players, had inched Rhee to his limits.*

# Thirty-Five
## *Boys Like Brothers*

L**ATER THAT DAY**, Rhee paced the length of his mother's vegetable garden, contemplating the shocking situation in which he was embroiled. "I can't believe these people are trying to kill me!" With the pieces of the puzzle still not fitting together, something was missing. *I wonder if the Dark Stranger knows more than he's telling. Come to think of it, we haven't seen him in a while.*

The complex web of chaos enveloping the two towns, and the continuous interference from all the different players, had inched Rhee to his limits.

Frustration had boiled over. Images of more serious protective measures popped into his mind. "If anyone comes around this house again I'll—" He slammed his fist into his palm. "Enough is enough!"

❧

Unsure of what the day would bring, the boys further adjusted to their heightened senses.

Jordan kept hearing noises that would not shut off.

Kinsu's eyes had watered, stinging all night.

Chase's hands were stiff with pain.

Rhee's nose gravitated toward foul odors.

Alex's tongue had swelled up, burning for an hour.

But time would not wait until perfect conditions arrived. It was all starting to add up and weigh down. Still, Jordan, Chase, and Alex met up on the walk to school.

"I told you guys it wasn't a good idea to go into the preserve." Alex swung his backpack from one shoulder to the other. "My tongue is so swollen."

Jordan rolled his eyes. "Well, you went, too, and here we are."

"You never even stopped to give me a chance to explain why we shouldn't have been there," Alex said.

Jordan glared at Alex. "When I looked back and saw you, you were way behind us. That was your opportunity to turn around, and you didn't."

"We could've at least talked it out."

Jordan threw his arms up. "Well, we didn't, so now what?"

"What do you mean by that, Jordan? It's okay for our lives to be falling apart?"

"Look, we're doing good by being out there. It's hard, but we're getting closer. You saw it. Those people need us."

Alex pointed at himself. "Hey, what about 'us' over here?"

"What? We're trying to shut it down, bro. We're watching out for ourselves, and you, Alex."

"I know, but I'm thinking about this all the time and Josie's on my back because I'm always distracted."

Jordan curled his lips. "Josie? Whatever..."

"What did you say?" Alex tossed his backpack to the ground and walked toward Jordan.

Jordan put his hand up. "Get out of my face, man."

Alex charged at Jordan and seared his palms into his chest.

"Hey, cut it out, guys!" Chase wedged between the two, walking Alex backward.

Alex snatched his backpack and pointed his finger at Jordan. "Watch what you say about Josie!"

Their argument had traveled quite a ways. Without realizing it, they had reached the campus and had put on a show for all to see.

A large crowd stared them down.

Chase was still situated between the two agitated friends. "Alright, let's go."

From a distance, the Dark Stranger listened, knowing he would have to intervene to set some things straight, so he mentally crafted his plan as the school day got underway.

❧

Chase spotted Jordan talking with friends after the last bell. He waved to classmates, then made his way to his friend.

"Hey, dude," Chase said.

Jordan glanced over his shoulder. "Hey, what's up?"

Chase looked around to be sure they were alone. "Is everything good?"

Jordan paused. "Yeah, it's all good. How about you?"

Chase gripped his phone. "I guess I could be better."

Jordan rolled his eyes. "What now?"

"I thought you were going to put a lid on Mason."

"I did. Why? Did you hear something?" Jordan asked.

"Diane told me she saw Mason crying at Billiards Park."

"What! Did he say something to her?"

"I think the tears spoke for themselves, bro."

Jordan lifted his forearms to his head, tensing his biceps. "I'm doing everything I can to keep things cool."

Chase stuffed his anxiety. "Alright... I'm with you."

A fist bump set them apart as the friends stepped along the path of faith, trying not to lose hope for the cause.

಄

Walking home the long way, Chase took notice of the nooks and crannies around the homes on his street. *Where would someone try to hide?* He tightened his fists with his house in view, peering over his shoulder on the last stretch.

Working his key into the groves, he crossed the threshold with a single aim: to do something for Diane. *Dinner. I'll make dinner.*

He laid his backpack in the entryway and walked to Diane's desk. He saw their mother's photo in a silver frame. *Don't worry, Mom, I'll take care of her. I'll do better.*

He kissed the photo and went to the kitchen, hunting for cans of chili, and hot dogs and buns. *I'm no gourmet, but this is definitely edible. Now, where are the chips?*

He swung an imaginary bat, recalling a quote from Jackie Robinson on one of his baseball cards—'A life is not important except in the impact it has on other lives.'

*Nunchucks circled her torso, slapping back, forth, up, and under while she remained focused and composed with her eastern, tomboy flair.*

## Thirty-Six
## *Who's That Lady?*

WITH A HEAVY RESPONSIBILITY on their shoulders, the boys did their best to stay the course. Although there was a layer of dissension, especially with Alex, they were as skilled as ever as their night progressed in Sandry Lake.

Almost immediately, Jordan could hear a voice. "Someone's telling his goons to stay organized, get their weapons, and fight in pairs." He tilted his head. "Dang! He just told them to get out. Sounds like he's punching his own men out the door. Not sure, but it's probably Druth."

Chase eyeballed the empty streets as they walked. "There aren't any residents out here right now, so that's a good thing."

Alex peeked into an abandoned building. "All clear."

"Where's it coming from, Jordan? What direction?" Kinsu tried to map out their moves. "We need to zero in on Dru—"

A chain rattled as he spoke. Loose pebbles dashed across the dirt, skipping toward them. Thumps boomed in the night.

Kinsu clenched his fist. "Keep it tight, guys." He and his friends got into formation, staying close, agile, and ready to fight.

Tall shadows swallowed the boys. From out of the darkness, nine thugs converged upon them, some with protruding shreds of metal in their hands.

Jordan threw his fists in the air. "Focus!"

"You're going down!" Saliva flew from the mouth of a goon wielding a spiked bat.

Rhee swept in and took his weapon, flinging it into the air. "I don't think so!" He and Chase punched him in both eyes, then in the groin.

One down, eight to go. They braced for the next.

Kinsu was pushed into the side of a building. He shook it off, ran toward a thug, and landed a Yoko Tobi Geri-style jumping side-kick on his head, knocking him out cold. "Feels good, doesn't it?"

Alex boxed with another, punching him in the torso and head, thrashing him with an uppercut. He knocked the thug down and stomp-kicked his ribs. "Say goodbye to your toy!" He smashed the thug's weapon.

With a furious brawl underway, both sides were on full attack with the boys teaming up on take-downs.

Casting a wicked smile at Jordan while he was distracted with punching and kicking, a thug snuck up on him, then swung a knife frantically. He drove his weapon into Jordan's arm, drawing blood and screaming waves of pain.

"Aaaah!" Jordan grabbed his arm. He spun around, trying to get eyes on his attacker.

Kinsu saw blood running out of his friend's arm. "Jordan!" He ran toward him but was blocked by a powerful hooligan.

In shock, without the net he assumed would always be there, Jordan stumbled and fell down an embankment, out of sight of the boys.

Everyone fought harder to get to Jordan.

Rhee was battling a goon. "Where'd he go?"

Alex managed to slip away as the furious boys launched a full-blown assault on the ruffians. Sheer frustration fueled their rage. Edgy emotions focused their moves in taking down two more of the goons.

Chase roiled over the attack on Jordan. "Has this gotten crazy or what?"

"No... but it's about to." A lady snaked her way onto the scene, observing each of the boys.

Kinsu's senses flared with each of her steps. "What the—"

Wasting no time in joining the brawl, she planted a sharp elbow on a thug's throat. Kicks to his stomach caused him to topple over in pain.

The thug rolled around crying, "Ugh!" A stomp to his head quieted him down.

She cracked her neck, smoothing her silky ponytail. "Who's next?" She ran toward a thug, ducking down, punching wildly.

"Aww, damn!" He took it in the groin.

"Did you see that?" Kinsu whispered, his eyes bulging out of his head.

Her fearlessness amazed the boys.

Staring her down, the last two thugs attempted to quell her scrap mastery, but she was just as tough and instinctual as the boys, if not more so.

She reached behind her back and pulled out slender black nunchucks. "Looking for your mommy?"

The chucks circled her torso, slapping back, forth, up, and under while she remained focused and composed with her eastern, tomboy flair.

"C'mon, let's go!" she shouted, the chucks bouncing in her palm, the small chain sending out an inviting, rhythmic chime.

"Go get that woman!" screamed one of the thugs.

A hooligan lunged at her. She rammed the chucks into his gut until he fell. She stepped up and over him, finishing him off with a whack to his head.

The last one backed up, looking for an escape.

"Where is he?" she said, speeding toward him. "Did you hear me? Where is he hiding?"

The thug backed away, frowning.

"Don't feel like talking? No problem," the woman said, her leg sliding through the air. A crushing, full-frontal kick sent the thug over the embankment, close to where Jordan had fallen a few minutes earlier.

Kinsu saw nothing but darkness over the edge of the bank. "Oh... my—"

The woman spun around, eyeing a tattered shipping bag on the ground. "Are you boys okay?"

She faced Chase, Kinsu, and Rhee, who weren't sure if they were next. Sniffing the area, she repeatedly licked her lips.

"We're... uh... good?" Chase replied.

Swooping up the bag, she ran toward the embankment. She leaped, spreading her arms elegantly, jumping off where Jordan had fallen.

She landed on top of the thug.

"Aaaah!" Dirt flew into his mouth.

"This is your last chance, buddy," she said, the white in her knuckles showing. "Tell me where he is."

The thug scrunched his lips tight.

"Okay, then." Her fist smashed into his chin. "Night, night."

Rhee's jaw hung low. "Was that for real?"

Kinsu was on his knees, peering over the edge of the bank. "Who was that lady?"

"C'mon, let's find Jordan," Chase said, scrambling down the embankment to find their friend.

Rhee and Kinsu stayed close behind. The loose pebbles unsteadied them, causing them to slide among puffs of dust from time to time.

Alex's senses roared as the woman came toward him. "Hey, who are you?" he said, applying pressure to Jordan's wound.

She softened her stance. "Let me help you." She ripped the shipping bag into strips and tied them around Jordan's arm. "Get his legs."

She slipped her arms underneath Jordan's, holding him tightly as she stood. Her firm thighs assumed the weight of Jordan's muscle and misfortune.

"What's going on?" Jordan moaned, hearing the woman as she and Alex carried him to a safe place. "Who are you?"

"He's lost some blood." She lowered him, tenderly touching his face and hair, staring at Jordan momentarily. "Watch over him. He'll be okay, just get him home."

"But what about—" Alex said.

She turned and disappeared into the darkness.

Chase and the guys ran toward Jordan.

Kinsu threw Jordan's arm around his shoulder. "All those pancakes and biscuits had better not cause a problem right about now."

Kinsu got Jordan to his feet.

"I know, he's heavy, so watch it." Alex planted his hands at an angle on Jordan's back.

Rhee looked over his shoulder. "Sounds like trouble." He repositioned himself to protect Jordan.

Footsteps advanced in the darkness. The Dark Stranger came out of the shadows, noticing the bloody bandage tied to Jordan's arm. "What happened?"

"One of those thugs stabbed him," Chase said.

"Well, look who's arrived. Where have you been?" Alex stared the Dark Stranger down. "You're here one minute and gone the next."

"I told you, I would be near—"

"'Near' is not the same thing as here... with us."

"I've been 'here' doing the same thing as you, Alex. Looking for Druth... fighting, watching over—"

Alex got in the Dark Stranger's face. "Really? Then how come we never see you?"

"This is a waste of time," Rhee said, the temperature of his voice rising. "Nothing's better. Nothing's changed. Jordan got stabbed and they're trying to kill us!"

The Dark Stranger could see Jordan growing weak. "It is changing. We're getting closer."

"Not close enough!" Alex yelled.

"Ouch!" Jordan's painful wound throbbed.

Kinsu began walking with Jordan. "C'mon, guys, let's get him home." He stopped and looked over his shoulder. "Wait a minute, there's something else. There was a lady. She was like us. Sniffing, licking her lips, beating up thugs."

*What did he just say?* The Dark Stranger's composure defied his racing heart, causing him to wrestle his breath. "I see."

In all of creation, there could be only one person to fit this description—Alina Alcaraz Olivas.

"She kept asking a thug, 'Where is he'?" Kinsu said. "I'm not sure who she meant. Maybe Druth?"

Walking with Jordan was a daunting proposition, so the Dark Stranger hoisted him upon his shoulders. At breakneck speed, they all raced back to Danville Heights.

༄

Everyone knew the need for an explanation of this incident was dreadfully imminent. The looming task of crafting a story out of thin air was not only sickening, but would place a deep wedge between Jordan and his father.

Alex was visibly despondent when they reached Jordan's house. He touched Jordan's shoulder and walked away.

"We couldn't have known it would come to this." Jordan looked the Dark Stranger in the eye, trying to lift the mood. "Don't worry, I can still play football." He prayed he would not wake his dad or Mason as he entered the house.

The boys watched as the garage side door shut quietly behind Jordan.

"He's getting bolder by the day," the Dark Stanger whispered to himself, his hands behind his neck.

Kinsu was close enough to hear him. "Who, Druth?"

Chase and Rhee turned around, listening.

"Who's getting bolder? What's happening over there?" Kinsu approached the Dark Stranger, grabbing at his cape. "With Jordan getting stabbed and that lady coming out of nowhere, you need to tell us what's going on."

"Understood. But it won't be tonight." The Dark Stranger sped off into the night, his cape billowing behind him.

Swirling air whipped Kinsu's hair. "Unbelievable!"

Chase and Rhee walked away, dragging their feet somberly. Kinsu stood on the pavement all alone with a horrible nag, still asking himself, *Who was that lady?*

*Jordan took a deep breath and faced the hallway, realizing he was on a death march to the kitchen where his dad and Mason were deep in pancakes and eggs.*

## Thirty-Seven
## *Perfecting a Lie*

GRADUATION at Danville Heights High School meant the older boys—Jordan, Rhee, and Alex—would soon begin college or careers. It would be a proper season of maturity for all of them... if they could stay alive.

Withdrawn from his friends and Josie, Alex reflected on the incident with Jordan. *That was too close. I hope he's okay, but I really can't take this anymore.*

Violence, uncertainty, and keeping secrets had taken their toll. These uncharted waters were stressful and choppy, and he wanted out. *That's it... I'm done!*

As Alex worked through his feelings, he did not realize destiny did not agree with him, and it began fighting him every step of the way.

ي

"I was out late with a girl and someone came up from behind and tried to rob us." Jordan practiced in the mirror. "When I fought him, he stabbed me and ran away."

Jordan swiped at the fog on the mirror.

"I got into a fight and someone stabbed me. I mean, me and this girl were walking, and see, her ex came up to me and tried to fight me. When I punched him, he pulled out a knife and stabbed me."

An early morning shower gave Jordan time to clean up, scheme, and rehearse for the dreaded conversation with his father. He knew there was no way a stab wound would go unnoticed.

*Man, this hurts. I hope I don't need stitches.* He had rewrapped the wound as best he could.

Jordan took a deep breath and faced the hallway, realizing he was on a death march to the kitchen where his dad and Mason were deep in pancakes and eggs.

Russell gave Jordan an intimidating stare through the thick silence. "Where were you last night?"

Mason's chewing came to a halt.

Jordan buried his hands in his pockets. "Dad, I'm okay, but I had an accident. I shouldn't have been out with that girl, but I had a fight with someone, and I... I got stabbed."

His eyes hit the floor.

"What!" Mason screamed, tearing up, running to Jordan.

Russell knocked his chair over. "Let me see!"

K.N. Smith

"Dad, it's not that bad, it just hurts a little." Jordan looked to his brother. "I'm okay, Bud."

"Where did this happen?" Russell asked.

"Not too far from school."

"You and I have already had this conversation!"

"I know, Dad. It won't happen again."

"You're damn right it won't. First, you're grounded. Second, get your shoes on! We're going to the hospital."

"Dad, I'm okay, it just—"

Russell put his chest in Jordan's face. "Jordan, as much as I love you, if I catch you in this much trouble again, you will see a side of me you never thought possible."

Biting his lip, Mason motioned to Jordan to tell their dad the truth.

"I'll speak to Officer Johnston about this." Russell's hands dug into his hips. "I can't believe this happened in Danville Heights!"

Despite the pain, Jordan was hungry. He eyed the pancakes, but the chance to distinguish the edge's crunch from the center's fluff had vanished as his dad's lecturing boomed in his ears.

"I said... get your shoes on... now!" Russell shouted.

Jordan hung his head and went upstairs to get his shoes.

"And by the way, don't forget our talk. This is bad enough, but with girls, you keep it covered up," Russell reminded Jordan from downstairs. "No diseases and no babies. You hear me?"

Air rushed from Jordan's lungs, brushing his lips. "Yes, I hear you."

Mason followed Jordan upstairs.

Jordan put on his shoes, then went into the bathroom to check the medicine cabinet for a fresh bandage. He could see tears in Mason's eyes, reflected through the last of the fog on the cabinet's mirror. His little brother's despair made him feel sick to his stomach.

Jordan's eyes welled. He touched a softly folded tissue to his face, which met a lonely tear of regret traveling down his cheek. Although the sun was shining on a beautiful day, pain had stricken the brothers within the deepest crevices of their broken hearts.

*The Dark Stranger spared no words. "You need to know who you are, and how you got here. I'll tell you what I know, and what we need to do. You have to trust me. You really don't have any other choice."*

## Thirty-Eight
# *What Happened to Mom?*

THE DARK STRANGER REFLECTED, contemplating the intersection of recent events. Sensing the boys would soon meet at the edge of the forest, he sought to dissuade them from going to Sandry Lake tonight. *If they'll just hear me out, they'll know more about who they are, and what they're destined to become.*

Although less energetic than before, four of the friends were on schedule, giving it another shot. Despite Russell's warning, even Jordan was present.

Alex was the lone holdout.

The Dark Stranger had already arrived. A hint of somberness hovered, but they acknowledged him in a respectful way.

"Thanks for being here," Jordan said.

The Dark Stranger spared no words. "You need to know who you are, and how you got here. I'll tell you what I know, and what we need to do. You have to trust me. You really don't have any other choice."

Kinsu had grown tired of the riddle. "We're listening."

"As for Alex, I'll deal with him later." The Dark Stranger gathered the friends, sitting them near him. "The incident in the preserve. I was there. I saw what happened to all of you. I've been through many things. Countless situations. Some resulting in unresolved pain. I know what you're going through. Seeing you was an awakening. I'm sure Alina felt it, too."

"Alina? Is that the lady we saw?" Kinsu asked. "How do you know her?"

"Yes, that's her, and we'll get to that." He patted Kinsu on the shoulder for reassurance. "She can feel you all."

The boys listened intensely.

"On a fateful night twenty years ago, Jordan, your mother, Talia—"

"What? How do you know about my mom?" Jordan asked.

"I'm getting to that, Jordan... please just listen. Your mother and her first cousin, Alina, went to the preserve late at night. Alina was from another city," the Dark Stranger explained.

"First cousin? I barely saw her, but now that I think about it, she does look like my mom." Jordan struggled to recall the images. "I might have seen her photo in one of our albums."

The Dark Stranger went deeper. "Talia, and someone named Joaquin, liked each other, so we all met at the preserve. Talia brought Alina. It was innocent. But over time, Joaquin became extremely controlling."

Heat rushed into Jordan's face.

"What you need to know is," the Dark Stranger paused to brace himself as much as the boys, "Joaquin *is* Druth."

With the story twisting and grinding away, the boys fixated on the Dark Stranger.

"Joaquin changed his name as he grew darker. He never gave his real name, so most of his followers call him, *him*, and sometimes, Druth. I once got close to him and his gang and heard them calling him Druth. But I wasn't close enough to stop him. And as much as it pains me to say this... Joaquin is... you see... he's my blood brother," the Dark Stranger said.

"What?" Jordan yelled, jumping to his feet, pacing in circles. "No way!"

"Floating lights, clicking noises, beautiful leaves. It was all there. What happened to you happened to us twenty years ago. We all received the gifts. Joaquin, another friend named Ross Dawson, Talia, Alina, and me."

"Man, I can't believe this!" Kinsu swatted fallen leaves, which shot through the air.

"We were all bound by fate. But after that day, Joaquin reveled in his new powers," the Dark Stranger said. "Joaquin never really tired, and he changed his mind about how his gift of touch should be used. He demanded more. He could easily pick locks with his fingers. He started stealing, fighting, and evading the law."

Chase shook his head. "Is that why you told us to stay together? Now it makes sense."

The Dark Stranger continued. "We failed to come together. Joaquin turned to the dark side and recruited Ross. They left Danville Heights after Joaquin caused trouble for our parents. I knew something was wrong. It was out of Ross's character to act that way."

Jordan was still pacing around. "I can't imagine what my mom was going through."

"Talia was sad, but moved on and later married your father, Russell," the Dark Stranger said. "It was hard for her because Alina never came back after the night she got her gift. Talia was dealing with a lot she couldn't share.

"Joaquin convinced himself he was worthy of all power, like he was trying to fill a black hole. Ross was a kind person, but he followed Joaquin. Then he killed Ross for his gift. The moment he died, his gift of sight transferred to us, and our eyes burned like hell for three days. Our eyes were inflamed, agonizing. We were nearly blind.

"When I learned about Ross's death, I vowed to fight Joaquin because Ross and I had practically been like brothers. I was actually closer to him than Joaquin, who had great difficulty in his adolescence.

"I saw Ross's transformation, wearing baseball caps to block the sun, and other changes. He had a good heart, but somehow, Joaquin got a hold of him. It hurts me that I couldn't save him." Reflections of pain contorted the Dark Stranger's face. His chin dropped to his chest.

"Guilt has a way of slowing us down. Being alone is just easier, but there is a great mission at stake. Reluctance had consumed me. But Ross would want me to nurture your gifts. He was the brother I never had."

Kinsu stared at the Dark Stranger. "What did you say? Baseball caps?" He saw himself in the Dark Stranger's words.

"I have seen the same in you, Kinsu. At times, light can show no mercy on sensitive eyes." Compassion filled the Dark Stranger's heart. "I understand the adjustments you are making, and I know it hurts."

"Well, I guess I don't feel so alone," Kinsu said.

"After killing Ross, Joaquin hid in the shadows. And the same thing happened when Talia died," the Dark Stranger recalled.

He remembered the deafening ringing. It had shot through their ears for three days. The pain had taken him, Alina, and Druth to the core of their souls.

"When we received Talia's gift of sound, we understood what the burning eyes had meant. We knew it was from Ross. They were both gone forever."

Jordan's watery eyes lacked movement.

The Dark Stranger shook his head slowly. "Talia had a hard time handling her gift, Ross's death, and the memories. She told friends that someone, or something, was haunting her. She started drinking to numb the pain.

"It was rumored that someone was standing on the side of the road when Talia crashed. The other driver survived, and from his description, it had to be Druth."

Jordan stopped pacing. "Please don't tell me that. Please don't—"

"If she saw him, she would have been scared," the Dark Stranger said.

It was the worst news of Jordan's life. "I've been looking into my mother's death. Something just didn't add up. She wasn't drinking when she died. I saw the police report myself. I called to speak with the other driver, Mr. Adams, but he had died just three months ago. I just can't believe it."

"Jordan, your mother would be proud of the man you're becoming." The Dark Stranger touched Jordan's shoulder. "You both share the same gift, which means it must be used to its greatest capacity."

"You've been dealing with this for twenty years?" Chase stared into nowhere. "This is so weird. It's hard to understand."

"Mark Grayson." The Dark Stranger stood. "That's my real name. But I haven't used it since Ross's death. Most of us left Danville Heights. Joaquin and I were declared missing persons. I still have the news clippings.

"The hardest part is that our mother went into a deep depression. Our father tried everything he could to console her, but nothing worked. They loved us equally, but Joaquin's emotions seemed to work against him constantly.

"Our gifts have changed over time. Weaker in some ways, more defined in others. Two of us are dead. We're not as strong because of Druth, but I can see, hear, and smell; Alina can see, hear, and taste; and Druth can see, hear, and touch; each with great power and intensity.

"I told you about the Naculeans. It's their nectar, their life-source, which brings the gifts," he continued. "Things went wrong for us but can go right for you if you stay together. They want to empower you to fight this evil."

The boys clung to his knowledge.

"Please... heed my words. I warned you about splitting up. Play with fate and all of you will suffer. Not to mention what will happen to mankind if Druth gets all the gifts," Mark said.

"We all had the same dream." Kinsu recalled the vivid warning. "We've been trying, but we need help. Like... every day until it's resolved. We can't do this alone."

"I failed to set things straight in the beginning," Mark said. "I'm sorry."

Overwhelmed by this new reality, the four friends were more deeply bonded for a higher cause. Accepting it would be their only option.

"I'm certain we can find Druth's hideout. You're already making great progress." Mark's eyes revealed a gleam of hope. "We'll find him. Let's plan it out."

And as the moonlight cast its glow upon them, the boys huddled with Mark, finding allegiance to their supernatural gifts, opening new vistas in a dreadfully complex predicament.

*The caregiver had explained to Juson that his mother's final, forceful exhale had crossed an invisible threshold. And at that moment the room was frozen, and she was dead.*

# Thirty-Nine
## *Divided*

**M**ISSING IN ACTION—a fitting description for the elusive Alex. Although despondent, he did not know his absence had weakened the group. He fought the urge to connect, to see his friends. *Maybe I should call the guys. No, forget it. It's more peaceful this way.* With their boyhood bonds buckling at the seams, there was no easy fix.

Being especially close to their oldest son, Alex's parents knew something was wrong, but gave him space and time to figure things out. Yet under the circumstances, that wouldn't last forever.

༄

"We all need a mental break from everything that's going on." Rhee ran his fingers through his golden hair. "It would be nice to just do nothing."

Jordan recalled the good times. "I remember all those fishing trips and barbecues when we were little."

Chase looked for shapes in the popcorn ceiling of Rhee's studio. "Yeah, things were simple back then."

Kinsu munched the last of his cheese puffs. "Just kids playing around."

"Rhee, remember when you got scared by my sister's cat?" Chase said. "You took off running and no one could find you!"

Rhee shook his head in amusement as laughter made its way through the air. "How could I forget?"

Being out at night, caught up in altercations, and maintaining a secret relationship with Mark went against their upbringings. The four friends searched themselves for a way to make it right.

"Now that we know the truth, let's hope things get better," Jordan encouraged the guys. "At least we have Mark to—"

Kinsu's vibrating phone distracted the group. His finger met the screen. "Hey, Dad."

"Kinsu, you need to come home." Juson's emotional voice coursed the airwaves.

Kinsu jumped to his feet. "Is everything okay?"

"I'm sorry to have to tell you. Grandma passed away. Her caretaker just called. We need to leave for Japan for the funeral, to handle her affairs."

"What? Grandma died?"

"She died in peace. We'll miss her so much."

The caregiver had explained to Juson that his mother's final, forceful exhale had crossed an invisible threshold. And at that moment the room was frozen, and she was dead.

Kinsu was anxious about interrupting the flow with the guys. "We have to leave now?"

"Yes." Juson placed his passport on the dresser. "It's time to come home and pack. We're leaving today."

Kinsu turned to his friends. "Okay, I'm on my way."

Sensitive to the situation while fearful of splitting up, they all knew this meant pull together or collapse, right then and there.

"We're sorry about your grandma. We'll walk you home." Jordan looked at the guys and jerked his head sideways. "You'll be back in no time. We'll be okay until you return."

"For sure." Kinsu stared into nothing. "But I'm out."

"What do you mean, 'out'?" Jordan asked.

"The beat-making contest. I made it to the last round. I'm one of two finalists, but there is one more challenge... tomorrow. All this pressure with Druth, no sleep, my grandmother just died, and now I can't finish the competition because I'm out of time and we have to leave. So... I'm out. There goes money for college."

Jordan felt Kinsu's pain. "Dang, man."

"Stuff happens." Kinsu dabbed his eyes. He put on his baseball cap to shield his eyes from the sun as his friends walked him home.

Each step carried the weight of a mile. Stretches of hope unrealized. Like cement blocks, Kinsu dragged his feet to his destination. They arrived to see luggage stacked on the porch.

Kinsu spoke beneath his breath. "Hang in there."

"You, too," Jordan said.

Juson slammed the trunk to signal the beginning of a long journey. The boys held eye contact with Kinsu through the car window.

Chase, Rhee, and Jordan soon faded from view, left behind to keep it together in the name of fate. And on cue, a subtle agony consumed the three amongst the warm winds in the peaceful town of Danville Heights.

*She ran to him, sinking into two decades of pain and resilience. He wrapped her with safety and assurance, unlike the uncertain waters they had both traveled, lost and surviving, torn and apart.*

# Forty

## *Fate of the Nectar*

RED PARTICLES ESCAPED the can's pressure as Jordan smashed his finger on the nozzle. Against the side of a building in Sandry Lake, the fine, even mist made its way through the alphabet, settling on 'GAME OVER'—a spray painted message to Druth from the three remaining friends.

Under a mass of smog, they continued serving the cause, making themselves known.

A shadow against the sky brushed the corner of Rhee's eye. "Hey, look over there." His fiery nostrils led the way.

Following the trail of an odor, he could see someone jumping from roof to roof, looking back at them.

"I've got the scent," Rhee said. "Let's go!"

They ran like lightning, catching up to the jumper.

Framed by a marbled moon, the figure made its way to a roof's edge and stomped three times. A rusty gutter shook, nearly detaching from the building.

It was Druth, who stared at Rhee. "I love your hair."

The boys slowed down, their shoes sliding sideways, digging into the dirt.

Noise from behind a cracked door spilled into the air. Someone swung it open with force, the doorknob blasting a hole in the wall.

Shiny earrings dangled from the lobes of Druth's men, matching the chipped silver-gray paint on the building. Foul breath escaped through their tooth gaps. Their ripped jeans hung low.

Moonlight bathed the boys as brass knuckles flew through the air, straight toward Chase, who ducked, but not fast enough. The knuckles clipped his head, which sent blood flying.

Rhee kicked a goon away from Chase. "You okay?"

"I guess so," Chase said. "I really don't have a choice right now, do I?"

Angry thugs towered above the noticeable loss of the boys' strength, weakened by the absence of Alex and Kinsu.

Druth sprung himself from the roof. Dust flew with a massive thud as his boots tore into the ground. The moments stilled on his march toward Rhee.

The blond hairs on Rhee's neck stood up. His biceps widened, his fingers curled under tight fists. With his knees bent in a fighting stance, he watched as Druth's hair blew in the wind.

Druth stood regal to his gang, turning to his men. "You know what to do."

He sped away as the thugs raged.

"Ugh!" Jordan took a few in the stomach.

The boys fought back. But needing to double up against the goons drained their energy.

A thug looked at Rhee, pounding his fist in the palm of his hand. "The blond one..."

Rhee's heart raced. *Are they talking about me?* Visions of the attacks on him and Alex flooded his mind.

"Looks like him to me," a hooligan said.

Chase held his pounding head. Jordan held his stomach. The hooligans surrounded the boys. "Hey, blon—"

*Whack!*

Alina's nunchucks smashed into the thug.

With more strength and grace than ever before, she whipped the hooligans, knocking them out cold. A small mountain of washed-up goons was left on the side of the road.

"Whoa... Alina," Chase said.

She turned to the boys, but a familiar scent touched her emotions, swelling her senses.

Sniffing and licking her lips, she moved in front of the boys, protecting them. "Who's there? Show yourself or you'll be—"

"Sorry?" Mark said, walking toward her, streaks of light cutting across his face. He removed his hood. "Alina, to see you here... it's a miracle!"

Twenty lost years rushed to the surface.

"Mark?" Alina froze, focusing her vision. "Is that you?"

"When Kinsu described you, I knew it was you. But it's still unbelievable." Mark could hardly believe the surreal reunion. "You're so beautiful and strong."

"I've thought of you so many times," Alina said, "wondering if you were okay."

His eyes touched every surface of her being.

She ran to him, sinking into two decades of pain and resilience. He wrapped her with safety and assurance, unlike the uncertain waters they had both traveled, lost and surviving, torn and apart.

"Have you seen your family?" Mark asked.

"No. After what happened, I never saw Talia or our family again." Alina dropped her head. "It hurts."

Mark held her tight. "I'm so sorry."

"And I know about Joaquin." Alina looked into his eyes. "He's been trying to find me, to kill me."

Mark's face grew red with anger at the thought. "Don't worry. We're on his trail. I'll explain later."

Jordan, Chase, and Rhee stood on the sidelines with mixed emotions.

"So, let me get this straight. You want us to deal with what you've been dealing with for twenty years?" Rhee looked back at the pile of goons who had been after him. "I'm the one being hunted. For what, my 'gift'?"

"It is hard to understand." Mark tried to reassure the group. "Have faith in—"

"In what, the nectar?" Rhee moved away from the others. "The source of all this pain?"

"Listen, Rhee," Mark sought to clarify his words, "it wouldn't be so painful if Druth—"

"If Druth what? If not him, then it's someone else. Where does it end?" Rhee picked up his stride. "Will my mother be in danger next?"

Mark reached out, his fingertips catching Rhee's shirt. "You don't understand."

Rhee jerked back, slapping at Mark's hand. "Not trying to, either!" Frightful memories filled his mind.

"Rhee, wait!" Jordan yelled.

"Didn't you see those guys staring at me… again?" Rhee ran away from Sandry Lake yelling, "If you're with me, then let's go take care of that stupid plant!"

Alina grabbed Jordan. "He's upset. Don't do it!"

"What if he's right?" Jordan wriggled away from Alina. "Getting rid of the nectar might make all of this go away."

"I've been here since this morning, fighting, tracking Druth," Mark said. "I closed down one of their hubs, cleaned it out completely. He's running. You just saw him, on the roof, in the flesh. There's a right way to handle—"

Jordan and Chase raced after Rhee.

"Oh, great, here we go." Alina kept pace with Mark, running to the preserve, resolved to watch over the boys to save them from total despair, yet lessons plagued the collective.

Rhee ripped through the forest, huge leaves blocking him at every turn. Jordan and Chase stayed close behind. With their senses burning, they came upon a huge succulent with a glowing center.

Blue veins in the leaves pulsed in the night.

"This has to be it." Rhee fumed at the sight. "Alex was right. We should have turned around when he first brought it up." He kicked at the glorious succulent. "I'm sick of these threats on my life!"

Chase and Jordan grabbed nearby branches and pounded the plant with their full strength. Tears met the darkness, glistening under the light of the Naculeans, who were watching the boys.

"It is time," one of the beings said.

Their floating became erratic, their feathered edges stood on end. Wisps of light left their bodies.

"Ouch!" Jordan held his ears, looking into the sky. Deafening clicks brought the boys to their knees.

"Stop! You will not destroy the nectar," a Naculean shouted. "We sense your pain, but this is not the answer."

A bright light covered the boys who were clutching their ears.

Chase saw the light, which looked familiar. "Who are you?" He heard rustling leaves, signaling the arrival of Alina and Mark.

"So, this is how you guide the young ones?" a Naculean asked Mark. "Has your hand not been on their shoulders?"

The painful sound waves multiplied.

"We have warned you too many times!"

"Please!" Mark pleaded. "They are upset and overwhelmed. I take responsibility. We are trying. Please stop!"

The Naculeans ceased clicking. Stilled yet exhibiting their force, they dimmed their lights slowly.

"Mark, what is this?" Alina grappled with memories of being in the preserve. "Are these the same beings that covered us with the light?"

"Yes, the Naculeans, the source of the gifts. They empowered us, and the boys. We carry their life-source in our veins. And so does Druth."

Rhee sat on the forest floor, his stomach muscles tight, his eyes wide with disbelief.

"We are here to promote peace," a Naculean said.

"It is our mission, our purpose."

"We protect the people and the nectar."

"Yet peace is needed within the peacemakers or destruction will soon follow."

"Druth must be stopped!"

"You are the only hope of the world."

"It is chosen."

The boys rubbed their achy ears, peeping in awe at the glowing beings.

"We understand," Mark said. "Alina and I realize our purpose. Despite all hardships—and there have been many—we respect our gifts. We know we are chosen."

Alina reserved her feelings about the Naculeans, searching herself for leadership. "Get up, boys." She extended her hand to them. "Mark and I will stay with the boys. We will find Druth."

Mark hugged Rhee, feeling his fear. "Be strong. We're in this together. We will protect you."

Alina turned to Jordan. "You look like your mother." She drew him close. "I can hardly believe my eyes and how mature you are. I'm so proud of you. Remember her sacrifice. Stay focused."

"It hurts to know she'll never come back." Jordan glanced over his shoulder at the Dark Stranger. "But I'm strong like her. I'll be okay."

"It's time to get you home for some rest," Mark said. "We must be ready for what's coming."

The Naculeans extinguished their lights and flew to the sky. But one light remained—the fluttering light ball.

It swirled around the group calmly, triggering the boys' recollection of their first time in the preserve.

The power of the moment touched Mark. "Come closer." His arms encircled the group. "We are in difficult times, but we must remember... destiny builds character for those who are chosen."

His words sunk into their hearts and minds.

Comforted by the stillness, each one surrendered to their power. Destiny swelled inside the preserve, which was no longer forbidden to those who were chosen to determine the fate of humanity.

*"I can't... lose her."* Alex's voice broke at the thought of losing Josie. Broken boyhood bonds crushed him further.

## Forty-One
# *Confrontation*

**M**ARK FINALLY KNEW his place in the boys' lives. Transformed over twenty years ago, he was incredibly strong, yet had limited powers because his group did not survive. *Still, we can do this. I am resolved with my destiny.*

Although successful with Alina's intervention, last night in Sandry Lake was tougher than it should have been. It would take all of them working together to win the war, inching closer with each passing moment.

From his cottage, he meditated upon his life and the lives of the original five. *Teaching the boys to look toward the future is critical if they're going to survive. We all have a mission to save mankind.*

He knew time was of the essence ticking louder with greater intensity as Druth made new moves in plain sight.

၄

A golden-orange sunset seeped through multi-colored leaves rising and dipping in the fall wind. Alex pushed himself, one miserable foot in front of the other, as he made his way home. *I missed another date. What excuse can I give Josie this time?*

He saw familiar territory—quaint shops lining a small commercial corridor, solar-lit umbrellas splashed across a restaurant row. *I miss eating there. Best pizza in town. Josie loved it. She'll probably go off to college without me. This is a mess. How did our signals get so mixed up?*

His mouth filled with fluid, a reminder of his friends and their plight. *Swallow it, keep moving.* Walking past a children's playground offered a momentary reflection of better times.

His home's chocolate and cream exterior came into view. Alex arrived to find a note from his dad—'We'll be back. Pull Mom's car into the garage.'

Alex revved the engine of his mother's car, parking it inside the garage. But when he turned it off, a shadow advanced from the darkness.

Alex's hand jerked, jingling the keys. "What the—"

"Your friends are worried about you. We're worried about you." Mark wrapped his hand around Alex's arm. "You must reconsider your actions."

"I can't do it anymore. Everything's wrong!"

"The reason it feels wrong is because you're fighting it. Don't think your friends aren't feeling the stress, too. It's a necessary adjustment."

"I don't know about that."

"Well, I do. If anyone would know, it would be me."

"I can't keep doing this to my girlfriend, not showing up for her."

"One day, you'll be able to tell her, and she will understand."

"She would never accept it! We're leaving Danville Heights. That's our plan."

"You cannot do that, Alex!"

"I can't... lose her." Alex's voice broke at the thought of losing Josie. Broken boyhood bonds crushed him further.

Mark understood the deep emotions swelling Alex's heart. "Destiny is not a choice. Seeing you boys tells me that. If we work together, amazing things will come. Please trust me."

Alex's eyes drifted. "It's hard."

"True, but you must focus your gift and reconnect with the others in order to reach your full potential."

Powerful sensations ran through Chase, Jordan, and Rhee, all sensing Alex, compelling them to see about their friend. They rushed to his house and found him with Mark.

Alex softened amongst the loyalty of brotherhood. "Hey, guys." Their presence brought him deep comfort.

Chase looked Alex straight in the eyes. "We're with you, bro."

"Alex, we need you. It will all work out," Rhee said.

Jordan hugged Alex tightly. "Boys like brothers."

Alex fought tears as he reconnected with Jordan, his pain evident to his boyhood friend, whom he loved.

Pulling together would be their only choice, with teamwork as the central element to define their incredible legacy.

Mark felt the emotions of the four friends. "I assure you, these gifts will take you many places, some rural, some urban. Just stay the course." He looked deep into their impassioned eyes.

With their strength and power poised for greatness, the group huddled to enlighten Alex on new developments, positioning them to become—'The Urban Boys'—the heroes fate chose above all others.

*Mrs. Perkins heard the commotion, sat on her porch, and rocked away. A light ball flew above her head, circling slowly, absorbing the emotions in the atmosphere.*

# Forty-Two
## *The Policy of Honesty*

SLICING INTO THE DIRT with a rusty shovel, Druth gloated over his secret hiding spot. "Socked away for a rainy day." Large bills, small bills. All stolen. He loved touching the bills, taken from banks and stores where he had wandered.

"Hey, boss," Omar said, standing a short distance from where Druth was hiding his loot, "we're ready. Just waiting for those punks to fall into our trap."

"Good stuff, Omar." Druth tossed the shovel, trying to hide it. "I'll catch up with you guys in a few minutes."

"Got it." Omar quietly inched closer to Druth, watching him bury a shiny metal box. He noted its location, then went to check on the goons who were ready for battle in the thick of the night.

❧

"I'm pretty sure I see it." Alina eyed a rundown building high on a hill.

Rhee helped pin-point Druth's hideaway. "I think she's right. I'm catching his scent."

"We'll have to come in from all sides," Mark said, painting a scenario for confronting Druth. "He knows we're here, so tomorrow we'll need to catch him off guard."

"Okay then... we're set," Alina said, "but let me show you something before we go. Stand back." She twirled her nunchucks. The air hummed through a dazzling demonstration of their fury.

The boys' eyes spun in circles.

"Wow!" Jordan mimicked her moves in the air.

Alina handed him the chucks. "Here, give it a run."

Alex ducked down, his hands shielding his face. "Don't crack yourself on the head, Bruce Lee."

Jordan instinctively commanded the chucks.

Chase enjoyed the entertainment. "Now, that's what I'm saying!"

"You're all doing great. Keep it up," Alina said. "Alright now, go and get some rest. Sleep as deep and as fast as you can."

Her assurance comforted the boys, but with the tension rising, the friends missed Kinsu.

"We need our boy back," Chase said.

"I know. He'll be back soon," Jordan said.

"For now, let's worry about a couple of other things." Mark projected a serious tone. "Rhee, Alex, unblock the roads. Jordan, Chase, find some food and drop it at the citizens' doors. Be quick!"

The tasks were accomplished with lightning speed, setting them on the road to Danville Heights, running most of the way, tip-toeing for the remainder.

လ

Now after midnight, Jordan reached the wooden steps leading to his front door. His feet moved with caution, treading lightly, but the last step presented a most feared barrier—an unamused Russell.

"Dad!" Jordan's heart jumped into his throat.

Russell stared into Jordan's eyes. The intense exchange instantly propelled father and son into a new realm.

"Where the hell have you been?" An animal-like growl escaped from Russell's mouth. "And if you tell me anything other than the truth, you will regret it. You'd better hear me!"

In recent days, there had been other parents at Russell's door dealing with the same. Enough was enough.

Jordan backed up two or three steps from Russell. "I can explain."

"What is going on?" Russell said. "And why are you and your friends out this late, night after night? I warned you—"

"Jordan, tell the truth." Kinsu came up the driveway, fresh from the journey with his family.

"Kinsu?" Jordan was happy to see his friend, but was bewildered at his timing and instructions.

Juson had arrived to the midnight encounter with Kinsu, his weight digging into the steps as he climbed. "It's okay, Jordan." He laid a reassuring hand on his shoulder. "It's time to be honest with your father. Kinsu and I have spoken in great detail. I know what's going on. Russell... we have a situation."

"Sometime this year, somebody. Twice I've asked what the hell is going on." Russell's biceps bulged out of his folded arms. "I'm not asking again!"

Sensing the confrontation, Mark and Alina rushed toward Jordan's house. Hearing Russell's anger, they hid in the bushes as the drama unfolded.

Mrs. Perkins heard the commotion, sat on her porch, and rocked away. A light ball flew above her head, circling slowly, absorbing the emotions in the atmosphere.

"Being away has given me time to think." Kinsu walked up the steps, pushing past Juson and Jordan.

"Now I understand our purpose, so I spoke to my father and told him the truth."

Russell cast an eye at Jordan. "You told your father what truth, Kinsu?"

"We weren't supposed to be in the forest, but we were. There was an accident, and we got hit by some kind of light or energy." Kinsu spoke with newfound confidence. "The energy came from the Naculeans, light beings. I mean, it came from their nectar in the preserve. And since then, our hearing, seeing, all of our senses are like... really heightened. Now our senses guide us to Sandry Lake, or to fight thugs right here in Danville Heights. It happens almost every night!"

"Light beings?" Russell looked shocked. "Wait a minute. You've been where?"

"Sandry Lake. And yes, it's bad, but we have to find Druth."

"Who?"

"Mark's brother, he's evil, now he's trying to kill Alex and Rhee for their gifts."

"Kill Alex and Rhee! Who in the world is Mark?"

"He used to live here."

"Where? In this house?"

"No, he used to—"

"Wait... hold on a minute. You've been going over to Sandry Lake for how long?"

"I don't know, like, a few weeks, maybe longer."

"Excuse me! And doing what, exactly?"

"Fighting thugs, helping citizens, trying to save the town from destruction, plus our own town. I don't know how else to put it, Mr. Parker. Mankind won't survive if we quit now!"

"Mankind! What?"

"If Druth gets all the gifts and powers, we're all dead. Okay?" Kinsu gulped on his breath, his eyes blinking wildly. "End of story. Gone. Finished!"

Juson and Russell shouldered the burden of disbelief, trying to process that the story could be true.

"I still can't believe it, Russell." Juson breathed deeply to settle his mind. "I know how you must feel. I'm still trying to grasp it."

With dishonesty shoved to the side, the boys were finally able to come clean.

"Well, you see, Mark is a… dark stranger. He watches over us," Kinsu continued, flapping his arms like Mark's cape.

"Dad, Mark told us the truth, even about Mom." Jordan stepped closer to his dad. "She knew Druth back in the day. I mean, Joaquin. Mark and Joaquin are brothers. They were in the preserve with Mom. She had the gift, too. That's why she was drinking. She couldn't handle it, but she wasn't drinking on the night of the crash. She loved us, Dad."

"She wasn't drinking—" Russell stared at Jordan, then became distracted by a shadow in the midst. "Alex?" He tried to hold on to Jordan's words while watching their friend run up the driveway.

"I could feel the tension, Jordan. I knew where you were." Alex was shocked in hearing about Talia for the first time. "I'm sorry about your mom."

"Thanks, man," Jordan said.

By this time, Mason was peeping from the front door. *Oh, dang. What's going on out there? Jordan is in deep stuff right now!*

"Dad, there's one more thing. Mom's cousin, Alina, is alive, and she's been out there with us." Jordan, mindful of the bullets flying at his dad, felt he needed to get it all out. "She's the one who wrapped my arm that night. She was in the accident in the forest with Mom a long time ago, and her senses guide her, too. And Dad, she's as beautiful as Mom."

Russell took a deep breath, his fingers squeezing his lips sideways. "This is just too much."

The light ball flew from Mrs. Perkins's porch and began twirling as Chase and Diane approached the group.

Russell felt overwhelmed. "What! You, too?"

"He was trying to leave the house, saying his hands were burning, and I said 'no way', so we talked and here we are," Diane said. "I can't believe this, Russell! Now I see why Mason was so upset."

"Mason knew about this?" Russell asked.

He turned to see Mason crouched, watching from the front door. Mason looked at Russell, then Diane, who had placed her hand over her heart.

*Poor baby*, Diane thought.

Mason slipped down a little further, hoping his dad would stay consumed with the confusion instead of him.

Also joining was a tired and confused Sandy. "What in the world is going on?" She was just as dumbfounded as the others. She had caught Rhee, who was in tow, as he had tried to sneak into the house.

And as the boys explained how Druth, Alina, and Mark had gained their additional senses, Juson lowered his eyes.

He recalled his and Della's venture into the preserve on that fateful night. He was now certain of what had happened—they were blind witnesses to Ross's death at the hands of Joaquin.

Juson's troubled thoughts spilled into the discussion. "We shouldn't have been in there."

Kinsu turned and stood face-to-face with his father. "Where, Dad?"

"In the preserve when we were young. I think your mom and I overheard Ross's murder. I'm pretty sure. No, I am sure we heard it."

"You and Mom? Dad—" Kinsu said.

"We kept quiet because we didn't want anyone to think we had anything to do with it. But now I know it was Joaquin. It had to be."

"Dad, you've kept this secret all these years?"

"The memory is still vivid, especially for your mom."

Kinsu thought back. "So that's why she was crying when we ran into the forest when we were little."

Russell rejoined the conversation. "Juson, you need to tell Officer Johnston about this right away."

Juson wiped the sweat from his brow. "You can rest assured, Russell, I will."

The boys carried on, their stories spilling into the night.

"I'm so sorry for keeping this from you, Dad," Jordan said. "But it's so bizarre, it was impossible to know where to begin."

"Is that why you were stabbed in the arm?" Russell asked.

"I didn't want you and Mason to worry." Tears fell from Jordan's eyes. "I'm really sorry for lying."

"I may not have shown it then, but my heart was crushed when you were stabbed." Mist filled Russell's eyes. "You and Mason are all I have."

Jordan wrapped his arms around Russell's strong, protective frame. "I'm sorry, Dad."

"I love you, son."

"I love you, too, Dad."

The light ball danced. Mark and Alina could see the flickering glow in the distance, bouncing around at Mrs. Perkins's house. They continued to observe from the shadows.

"It's time," Mark said. "It had to come to this, but at least it's out in the open."

Alina's eyes fixed on Russell and Jordan, the family she had never known. "It will work out in their favor."

Mason looked to see the light ball flying around. *Whoa! I remember seeing that thing.*

Mrs. Perkins observed the actions and emotions of the group. After a few tiny clicks, the light ball zoomed to the sky.

"Who's that woman over there?" Alina stretched her neck to get a glimpse of the silver-haired lady. "The one in the rocking chair."

"That's Mrs. Perkins," Mark said, "she's the one... who sees and hears much."

"It's pretty late for her to be up."

"It's no coincidence. She can talk to the light ball."

"Well then, the Naculeans will be well informed."

"At least we can be satisfied with the boys' honesty and integrity. They just need to be ready for tomorrow. There will be no turning back," Mark said.

The families were given little time to absorb this newfound reality before the boys would have to race off yet again. With the angst of discovery no longer a threat, they were poised to become the victors they were destined to be.

Back together, and now emotionally unimpaired, the boys felt stronger than ever under the watchful eyes of Mark and Alina. Nightfall would chase the new day, so there was no time to slack as they prepared to embrace their fate—one city, one thug, one villain at a time.

*They moved in sync. But it only took a few steps for their senses to flare as they saw numerous thugs running behind them.*

# Forty-Three
## *A Ruthless Brand*

SMALL, FRAIL HANDS carefully folded the remnants of his vast possessions, which were stuffed into a tiny bag. Seeing no other option, he had planned to slip away during the night in order to escape in search of a new life.

Stripped of what was rightfully his, he could take no more. The ruffians had robbed him, beaten him, and had left him for dead. The faithful citizens of Sandry Lake, who had found him lying by the side of the road, had brought him to safety. With barely enough to keep themselves going, they had fed him, nursed him, and shielded him from further harm.

Stanley Martin, a once-prominent attorney who had relocated to Sandry Lake for its peace and quiet, was now a skinny man of no means. He remembered wine, parties, and midnight toasts shared with colleagues and friends.

For this town to be overtaken by shameless greed was unthinkable. With the citizens asleep, he snuck away with only a shred of the dignity he once had.

❧

With the wheels of his cruiser grinding in the rubble, Officer Johnston drove to the edge of town. From earlier reports, he knew there was trouble in Sandry Lake, but it was out of his jurisdiction and he was cautious of proceeding without permission.

Stepping out of his cruiser, he reached into his pocket. His hand lifted a yellow stickie note, which was bright against the dark sky.

Having read the notes many times, he wondered who had written them and why the author had been so secretive. *Come on, give me a clue. Give me something!* And without a choice, patience took the lead as he waited in the pit of the night.

❧

With his finger tapping a chaotic beat, Druth plotted a final attack upon the boys. *They'll be back soon, but they won't make it out this time.*

Complicating matters was the fact that he could sense Mark and Alina. Besides the boys, there could be no other explanation as to why his senses were so acute and burning.

"If they want to play, we will play..." Druth nodded slowly, his foot moving to the wild beat, "...one final game."

❧

On the way to Druth's evil assembly, two thugs ripped through an apartment building to see if there was anything more to steal. Stanley Martin was walking down the road when he heard the commotion. He ducked into the brush.

Crashing and thrashing the place, the thugs showed no mercy in ripping off doors, overturning furniture, and slicing through mattresses.

Stanley looked out and saw an opportunity to run away. Fear propelled him like a bullet train, dust flying under his feet.

The thugs saw Stanley rush by with his tiny bag swinging like a chandelier. "Hey, get back here, you!" one of them shouted.

Face forward, Stanley ran with all his might. He met the darkness with open arms, running faster to soar to freedom.

The hooligans had their marching orders—continue wreaking havoc on the town and stomp out the boys. "Aww, forget him. Let's get this stuff over to *him*," a thug said. With an about-face, they were on their way to appease the sad, ruthless Druth.

ॐ

The operator adjusted her new earpiece. "Danville Heights Police Department, may I help you?"

"This is Bill Ganstone, I'm a Security Officer at Sandry Lake. We've got a situation!" His face, wrought with tension, twisted constantly. His hand dug into his side. "I've been stabbed. We need your help right now!"

"Sir, you're the third person to call in the last few minutes, so the cell towers must have been refreshed." The operator was amazed at the volume of activity on the switchboard. "One moment, please."

"Please... hurry!"

"Yes, sir." She flagged down the Captain on duty, handing him the receiver.

"Captain Michaels here," he said.

"Sir, we need your help." The officer winced in pain. He held his side, trying to stop the bleeding as he peeked around the building to see if he'd been followed. "Our commanding officers are either dead or missing. Someone stabbed me. We're overrun by criminals. We need assistance!"

The Captain stretched the coiled phone cable, tapping on the interview room door, signaling for an officer to assist. "What's your location?"

"I'm sitting outside the main utility building on 4th and Central. We lost power. We tried to contact you, but—"

"Hold tight, we're on our way."

"Oh, thank goodness... thank you, sir!"

With a desperate sense of relief in his heart, the Security Officer handed the cell phone back to the small, frightened man who had stumbled upon him only minutes after he was attacked by a vicious goon.

It was Stanley Martin. Against all odds, he had managed to hide a cell phone in his boot, powered by one of his stashed batteries.

When he ran into the Security Officer, nearly knocking him down, they scrambled to call for help. It was the golden ticket to deploying officers from another jurisdiction.

"Thank you, Stanley. You don't know how much this means," the officer said. "I hope they arrive soon."

"Of course. I appreciate your bravery, sir." Stanley sat with the officer, checking on his wound. "But I'm sorry, I can't take it... I need to keep going. It'll be just a few minutes. Just stay here and be real quiet."

Although still terrified, Stanley was determined to find a new life as far away from Sandry Lake as possible. He grabbed his tiny bag and took off into the night.

౨ం

The operator continued putting her skills to work. Lines two and three lit up, vying for her attention. "Wow, can you believe—"

"Captain Michaels, is everything okay?" Juson asked, peeking from the interview room, having been interrupted during his official statement regarding the murder of Ross Dawson.

"Sorry about that, Mr. Yamada." Captain Michaels said. "We'll soon find out."

"I realize it's late, but I just had to come down here. Seems like there's a lot going on lately."

"Indeed, Mr. Yamada. Indeed."

ॐ

"Calling all units, calling all units. Be advised, Security Officer down and in need of assistance in Sandry Lake." The dispatcher's voice traveled through Officer Johnston's cruiser. "Respond Code-3 to 4th and Central. If any units are close, please respond, Code-3."

"Check. Responding from Billiards Park, en route, Code-3." Officer Johnston stuffed the yellow note into his pocket. As he shifted the car into reverse, his eyes met the rearview mirror. *Who is that?* He was startled to see a group of teenagers speeding by, heading north.

He leaned out the window of his car, focusing as hard as possible, considering the wild blur of their furious sprint. *What are they doing out so late?*

By the time he had gathered his thoughts, they were out of sight. He dug into the steering wheel, spun the car around, and mashed the pedal, speeding after the runners toward Sandry Lake.

৸৹

Four units flashed red lights, illuminating the neighborhood, including Mason's bedroom window. He flew out of his bed, looking outside to see police cars winding through the streets.

Mason lit up, grabbing an unopened pack of yellow stickies, lavishing kisses upon the wrapper. "I knew they would find the notes!"

৸৹

Ready for action, Mark, Alina, and the boys arrived in Sandry Lake to make it known this reign of terror was going to stop.

"Stay together. Stay focused," Mark said.

"Go for the limbs first." Alina tightened her ponytail. "Get them down quickly. Do less fighting. Instead, be clever. There will be lots of them tonight."

They moved in sync. But it only took a few steps for their senses to flare as they saw numerous thugs running behind them. Practically tripping over one another to get to the boys, the goons advanced with Olympic-level speed, swarming like ants upon the group.

Taking Alina's advice, they zeroed in on limbs, breaking and cracking at every turn.

Alex and Rhee ran around several of the thugs, dizzying them. From behind, they locked their arms underneath the thugs' arms, reached up, and grabbed their throats. Hoisting upward while choking them, they cracked the thugs' arms at the shoulders, dislocating them from their sockets. Pain caused the thugs to be immobilized, and they were easy to kick to the side.

Alina waved them on. "Keep going, guys!"

With jump kicks to the goons' knees, the boys chopped and punched endlessly.

Alina swung her nunchucks to the backs, sides, and tops of heads, left and right. She cracked ribs and chuck-slapped the thugs with all her strength, as her smooth ponytail flowed beneath the moonlight.

Mark had a ruthless brand of his own. His presence alone caused some of the thugs to retreat. He went after them first to get the obviously fearful ones out of the way.

Spinning around, he side-kicked one after the other so hard, Jordan could literally hear the breath leaving each one as they crashed and burned into a sorry pile next to the goons with the broken arms.

The remaining few were kicked, jabbed, and stomped into oblivion until he appeared satisfied with the sickening, but necessary, crackdown. Void of emotion, Mark commanded the group. "We're done here. Let's go."

With that group of rowdy losers swept and left for the morning trash pickup, they were back on track to get the evil Druth.

*And just that fast, Druth made his move on Alex, attacking him with every fiber of his being, furiously moving about to get to Jordan.*

## Forty-Four
# *An Unpromising Proposition*

THE WINDING MESS leading to Druth's hideaway was full of weeds and trash, setting the stage for a nasty discovery. Sprinkled throughout the area, Druth's guards sent out their foul stench, detected by Rhee. "We're getting close. I smell their filthy odor."

As they navigated a steep hill, a ruffian jumped at them swinging knives, reminiscent of the attack upon Jordan.

Kinsu sped toward him, knocking the weapons away. "Not this time!" He teamed up with Mark, with one in front and one behind, lashing away until the goon rolled down the hill unconscious.

They weren't playing. Their lives were at stake, not to mention two towns and all of humanity. 'Onward' was the agreed-upon mantra as others tried to thwart them, only to encounter vicious counterattacks.

"We're here. I can smell Druth," Rhee said, recalling the rooftop taunt where the wind had carried Druth's foul essence, which was shoved into his nose.

Now at the top of the hill at Druth's hideaway, Jordan, pushing the door open, observed the mess. "This place is so creepy."

Strewn with stinking, rotten food, the place had thick cobwebs plastering the wall. Piles of trash disgusted the group. Rhee and Mark bore the brunt of the sour odor, nearly overwhelmed as they held their turned stomachs.

"A box of toys?" Jordan examined a set of colorful blocks made fit for preschoolers. "Is there a baby in here somewhere? Looks like Druth had been stacking these up."

He kicked at the junk on the floor and was struck by an image hiding beneath a pile of papers—a high school yearbook photo of his beloved mother, Talia.

Druth had kept the photo for over twenty years.

Jordan showed the photograph to Mark. "At least now it will be in the right hands." He released his grip slowly, achingly, from the image, putting it in his pocket.

Across the room, a large map covered with notes had been pinned to the wall. "Danville Heights. Sandry Lake. Lavender Quarry." Mark examined the fine geographic details. "So this is the master takeover map."

Streets and sidewalks, roads and rivers. A bullseye marked the Danville Heights Central Union Bank.

Mark studied the layout. "He's trying to take over the whole region. Blocking roads, shutting off power. Now it makes sense. He thinks our parents favor me when they do not. Joaquin was always so difficult, it made him dark inside. I excelled in some areas where he did not. It didn't mean I was favored."

Mark leaned in to see the X over his parents' home.

"Using his gifts to make our parents love him proves he's delusional," he said. "He's trying to get back at me by boxing them in so they'll have no choice but to listen to him. Over my dead—"

"I see someone!" Chase felt warmth in the room, noticing the back door had been swung open. "Whoever was here just left"

A shadowy figure was getting away.

"We defeated his men. He's all alone." Mark made his way outside. "He must be running toward the Stanton Bridge. Come on!"

They ran so fast their feet barely scraped the earth, trying to catch the figure before it could get across the bridge and into the bordering town of Lavender Quarry.

Jordan and Alex led the way, but Rhee tripped over a concealed, extended leg and flipped, smashing into Chase. The two scraped their way down a hill and were instantly out of sight. Screeching to a halt, the group searched for them in the darkness.

"What happened?" Alina scanned the area with her powerful vision. "Where are they?"

Jordan focused his gift, listening for movement. "I'm not sure. I don't hear them."

Mark charged into the brush to find them. "Keep going!"

While the others were absorbed by the distraction, Druth snuck in from behind, swinging a wooden bat.

"Watch out!" Alex screamed.

With a twitch to the right, Druth cracked Alina in the head, then swung left, smacking into Kinsu's skull.

Both writhed in agony, sliding down the hill.

A furious Alex struck a fighting pose. "Coming up from behind?" He spat and stepped to Druth. "How brave!"

Druth flung the bat.

Alex and Jordan witnessed the lowest of the low. Druth wore his dirty habits all over his sleeves. His filthy hair and layers of grit were practically shoved into their faces.

Druth looked at Jordan. "You want some, too?"

Jordan curled his upper lip. *Disgusting...*

And just that fast, Druth made his move on Alex, attacking him with every fiber of his being, furiously moving about to get to Jordan. "It's the end of the line for you, boy!"

Trading kicks, punches, and jabs in a death-style match, Alex and Druth fought at a dizzying pace.

Jordan moved in and punched Druth in the ribs, then took an elbow to his face. He stumbled back and fell with his hand over his eye.

Druth struck Alex and pinned him to the ground, digging his hands into Alex's neck. Alex saw a rage in Druth's eyes, a sinister well of greed fueling him to unleash his fury.

Druth leaned close to Alex. "He's trained you well, good soldier. Did you bring me a gift?" He hoisted his weight, lengthening his arms, pushing into Alex.

Alex dug into Druth's wrists, pulling, a deep red filling his face. His heels slid across the weeds as he squirmed.

Jordan got back to his feet, his eye watering, and reverse-kicked Druth in the head—a move he had learned from Mark.

Druth toppled, sliding away from Alex. But he threw his arm forward and grabbed Alex as he rolled. He stood and flung Alex, forcing him down a hill and into the brush.

Druth shook it off and walked toward Jordan. "Well, well, Talia's little boy." He tackled Jordan, wrestling him.

Jordan fought back violently, doing damage, punching Druth in both ears for stealing Talia's gift. "Son of a—"

Mark came up the hill, swinging at Druth, delivering crushing blows, causing him to spew blood from his crusty mouth.

Druth came back with hefty punches. "There you are in the flesh." He stepped back, catching his breath. "It's so good to see you again... brother!"

"This ends now, Joaquin!" Mark shouted, shocked at the dramatic changes in his only sibling.

"If you only knew. This is only the beginning!"

"You're right. It's the beginning of *your* end. Brother or not, this has gone too far!"

Druth laughed at the thought. "It's time to play, brother." Blood spilled from between his lips. "Time to stack the blocks and watch them fall!"

Druth took off running toward the Stanton Bridge.

Mark ran and caught up to him on the bridge. Old, flaky boards shifted under his brawny frame, causing the bridge to sway.

And as the callous Druth had hoped, they were in a perfect position for the ultimate showdown: brother-to-brother, hand-to-hand, good against evil.

※

A shovel met the earth, finally hitting a prized target—a metal box filled with cash.

"Jackpot!" Omar had discovered Druth's secret hiding spot. "I thought that's what that jerk was doing."

He dug up the box and ran off in another direction. Using one of the takeover maps, he plotted his way out of Sandry Lake, taking with him a car, the cash, and a trunk full of food. "Good riddance... *boss*." With loyalty nowhere to be found, Omar was ecstatic to be in the wind.

ॐ

Officer Johnston pulled into Sandry Lake. "I don't believe my eyes!" Broken glass, trash, and loose boards with protruding nails littered the area. And of all things, piles of broken down thugs lay on the side of the road.

Units rolled in with officers taking a moment to survey the shocking sight.

"It's worse than I could have imagined." Officer Johnston saw nothing but dilapidation. "Desperation is an understatement!"

He dove in to get to the bottom of things.

"Okay, you two, respond to the Security Officer at 4th and Central, and you two, follow me," he said. Winding up a steep hill, the cruisers' lights swept through the thick brush. He stared through the windshield. "People hiding in the bushes at night?"

Red lights encircled a group of people. It was Chase, Rhee, Alina, and Kinsu. Chase and Rhee had found their way to Alina and Kinsu, who had fallen after being whacked by Druth. They were tending to their injuries when the officers arrived.

Officer Johnston's heavy boots met the earth. "Well, I'll be danged." He was firmly eye-to-eye with Alina and the boys. "Kinsu Yamada. Is that you? What in the world is going on?"

Kinsu was still coming to. "Um... yes... sir?"

Unable to duck or hide, Chase and Rhee faced Officer Johnston. With the other officers looking after Alina, the boys broke it down.

"Well, uh... Officer Johnston, this has been going on for a while. It started in the preserve with some kind of accident, with the light beings. I mean, the nectar. Then we started coming over here." Rhee grew animated, his arms flailing. "But that's not the worst of it. Druth's been trying to kill me!"

"But they came into Danville Heights first," Chase clarified. "Did you see those thugs on your doorstep?"

Officer Johnston recalled the tags that had been tied to the hooligans. "Thugs on my doorstep? That was you? Well, I'll be—"

"This town is filled with goons, or what's left of them." Chase picked stickers off his sweatpants and out of his afro. "We're trying to save humanity. Sir, we've been stressed out, battling thugs almost every night!"

Officer Johnston stepped closer to the boys. "What! Just the three of you?"

"No, Alex and Jordan are here, too, and we have... you see... well, we have... a guide," Chase said.

"A guide? What the heck do you mean, son? What guide?" Officer Johnston's hat tilted to the side, his brow crinkled yet again.

Rustling could be heard as Jordan came out of the darkness, wandering around in the greenery. "Alex, where are you?"

"Jordan Parker?" Officer Johnston said.

Jordan's shocked eyes met Officer Johnston's. "Sir?"

"Does Russell know you're over here?" Officer Johnston straightened his hat and moved toward Jordan to be sure it was him.

"Well, sir." Jordan thought through recent hardships and the painful honesty imparted to his father. "Actually, he does."

As they stood face-to-face, Alex's panicked voice shot through the tall grass. "They're up on the bridge. Somebody... go!"

Jordan and Officer Johnston broke the stare down.

Jordan grabbed Alina's nunchucks as he took off. Officer Johnston followed him, sprinting toward the Stanton Bridge.

Jordan quickly passed Officer Johnston, who was still trying to absorb what appeared to be an incredible, mysterious mess.

ॐ

Now approximately at the middle of the span, Druth flashed his grin at Mark. "I knew this day would arrive."

Thick tension gripped the brothers. Mark lunged forward, punching Druth in the torso. Druth whooped on his brother with anger, landing an uppercut on his chin.

"It was always supposed to be me, not you." Druth was eerily gratified in his mayhem. "I'm coming back to earn their love. You're up against the ropes, brother, there's nothing you can do!"

Mark seethed. "You listen to me, Joaquin. Stay away from them—"

"Or what?"

Mark eased Druth further down the bridge, which was now swinging ferociously. "Trust me, you don't want to know!"

Druth lunged forward and cracked Mark in the eye, forcing him to misstep. Mark's foot punched a hole in the bridge, causing him to nearly fall through.

Mark grabbed onto the sides of the bridge. While he was down, Druth kicked him in the face and stomped on his hands. He stood over his brother with a twisted sense of power. He took long, deep breaths as though he was soaking up the universe.

Mark mustered the power to punch out the cracked boards underneath Druth, causing him to fall, barely hanging onto the bridge.

"And they said you were the smart one," Druth said, unfazed. "You should've listened to me and come with me."

"What happened to you, Joaquin? It didn't have to come to this." Mark was unable to find the Joaquin of his childhood in his brother's eyes. "And don't think we don't know about Ross and Talia. You killed Ross for his gift. You distracted Talia on that road. She crashed and died because of you. You're going to pay!"

"Dreaming is a good thing," Druth said. "Keep dreaming. I *will* have all of the gifts. All of the power!"

In a miraculous feat of strength, they both managed to get back on the bridge.

Jordan and Officer Johnston stood at the foot of the bridge. A floating light ball danced above their heads. Officer Johnston tried to swat it, but it circled around Jordan and blew a puff of light in his face.

"Whoa..." Jordan inhaled the burst of energy from the fluttering being. Soft clicking noises filled the air.

Officer Johnston looked into the dark, mysterious sky. "Wait... I know that noise." He stood with his hand over his revolver. *Let me think. It would be 20 minutes before K-9 could get here. Or maybe we can...*

Jordan broke away, racing across the bridge, running up from behind Mark screaming, "Get down!" His clutch revealed Alina's sleek nunchucks, which were swinging lividly.

And when Mark ducked, Jordan jumped over him, whacking Druth in the temple and across the face, causing him to flip over the side of the bridge. Druth's long hair flew through the air. Coins escaped from his pockets.

And with one hand, he caught the bottom rail.

A wild and angry river beckoned far below.

"Pull me up, boy!" Blood continued to trickle from Druth's mouth.

Wind tore through the scene. Dark masses slid across the sky, aligning, resembling a pair of striking eyes. Blue-green sparks shot through the air, blending with the charcoal mass. Jordan looked up, fixated on a dramatic optical illusion, the epicenter of his origin—his mother's eyes—beaming at him in the pit of night.

An echo, sounding like a deep version of Mrs. Perkins's voice, billowed through Jordan's ears—'Respect your destiny.' He felt the power of the nectar as his grip tightened around the chucks.

Although he was angry over his mother's death, he had not an ounce of revenge in his being, but he knew his place in the greater scheme of life. Jordan swung the nunchucks, landing a powerful blow across Druth's knuckles, which forced him to let go.

"I just wanted them to... love... me!" Druth screamed, spitting blood, his eyes meeting Mark's. But at that moment it was far too late for redemption.

And the angry river suddenly looked welcoming as it prepared to receive the evil Druth, who was screaming and twisting as though he was trying to grab everything on the way down.

As fate would reveal, Druth was exhausted and defeated. His cries billowed through the air to silence as the era of darkness in Sandry Lake faded behind a most calculated curtain of gloom.

*And like an eagle with wings spread, the boys poised for a soaring flight. With Mark and Alina, they were embraced by the deep night, having been missed by the late evening's elements, and because they were needed in other places.*

# Forty-Five
## *A Soaring Flight*

**A** GLAMOROUS ROW of blue hydrangeas met the guests as the evening began. Glowing lights, decorative linen, and a five-star worthy spread filled the garden. Families gathered for a celebration of sorts, with the boys on center stage.

Kinsu's beats boomed in the background. In appreciation of the beautiful setting, the five friends relaxed, knowing their secret was safe.

"I'm sorry for all the drama," Alex said, as his fingers intertwined with Josie's. "We still have our dreams. We can still have a great life. No, wait... we *will* have a great life, together."

"I know, Alex." Josie planted a kiss on his cheek. "Where there's a will, there's a way, right?"

Alex kissed Josie on the lips. "Definitely."

Jordan and Kinsu inspected the rich desserts.

Kinsu chose the chocolate mousse. "So much has happened. I never would have guessed."

"I know. It's a new way of life for all of us, but one day at a time." Jordan sliced into his cheesecake. "That's as fast as it goes for me, anyway."

"There's so much more we can learn from Mark. Can you imagine being out there like that for twenty years?"

"He's the real deal." Jordan licked his fork. "Maybe we'll be as strong as he is someday."

Kinsu nodded. "Alina's amazing, too. But man, I wouldn't want to be on her bad side, getting chuck-slapped upside the head."

"Ooh, seriously!" Jordan said, rubbing his head.

"Mark told me that sometimes destiny has a unique way of alerting us to all possibilities." Kinsu recalled the day he thought he saw something miles away from Mr. Knowlton's class. "He said to keep an open mind to greater experiences in life."

Jordan tapped his fork against his head. "That's some poetic stuff right there, man."

Kinsu raised his hand, high-fiving Jordan. "For real!"

Chase and Rhee stood to the side, practicing moves.

"You throw their arm back, open them up, and then punch." Rhee demonstrated his instructions.

"If you really want to do it right, you grab their arm when they punch." Chase pulled on Rhee to make his point. "You pull them in, get 'em down, then punch."

"Please! I've seen Mark do it lots of times. You need to up your game, Chase."

"Wait a minute... forget punching." Chase puffed his chest. "I need a cape. When do I get a cape?"

Rhee rolled his eyes. "This is just hopeless."

Realizing a new paradigm, Sandy and the other parents bonded in new ways, reflected in well-earned glasses of sparkling wine.

"I got the promotion at the bank," Sandy said. "Believe me, Della, the extra income won't hurt, you know?"

"I hear you. That's the best news." Della raised her glass. "Congratulations!"

"Thanks. You know, we've been living amazing lives and didn't even know it. Look at our boys."

"Can you believe it?"

"I think so, but it's bizarre, hard to believe. Looking back, those subtle clues now make sense, but you couldn't tell then. I'm just glad they're all safe."

Bringing a contribution to the affair, Mrs. Perkins sat one of her award-worthy buttermilk pound cakes on a table. Her faithful devourers could hardly wait.

She gave Sandy and Della a comforting wink.

"The boys will be okay, trust me," she said, a faint glow filling her eyes, reflected from a tiny friend—the fluttering light ball floating in the sky. "Now, where are those troublemakers?"

With the celebration underway, Russell called for a toast. "Because there's really no way to describe these recent events, we just want to say we love our boys and want them to be safe."

Cheers filled the party.

Rhee raised his glass, but only to watch it crash down. "Whoa—" He stepped back, examining the tiny shards shimmering in the glow of the garden lights.

"Honey!" Sandy rushed over to check on her son.

Rhee looked at his mother and turned his head sideways. With a choppy exhale and deep inhale, he moved toward the backyard gate.

Jordan listened intensely.

Kinsu blinked his eyes.

Chase cracked his knuckles.

Alex's mouth began to water.

Squeaky hinges elevated the tension as Mark and Alina entered the yard. Instinctively, Russell rushed to shield Jordan.

"Dad, it's okay," Jordan said. "They're with us."

Russell stared at Mark, but then offered a nod of reassurance. "You must be Mark. Thank you for watching over Jordan."

"You've raised an excellent son." Mark reached out to shake Russell's hand. "It's me who ought to be thanking you."

"Me, too." Alina stared into Russell's eyes, imagining the pain he had endured over Talia's death.

"Alina," Russell said, touching her arm. "I can't believe it. Jordan was right, you do look like Talia."

"Don't worry." Alina embraced Russell, trying to ease painful memories. "I'll stay close to Jordan."

"It means everything, thank you," Russell said.

"And where is Mason?" Alina's eyes swept through the waves in Mason's hair. "I bet that's him over there." She knelt, opening her arms for a long-overdue hug. "I hear you're a real hero."

She gave him a special kiss.

Mason melted into her embrace. "Aww, Alina."

"I know you worry about Jordan, but he's strong and capable. You'll be the same one day."

"Will you come to our house for a movie night?"

"I sure will."

"A zombie movie night?"

Alina smiled warmly. "Most definitely."

The festivities had warmed their hearts. But it was time. The dark night had called to the boys.

"Excuse us." Jordan nodded to his dad. "Time to go."

Russell hugged his son. "Be careful, Jordan." He slid his fingers through Jordan's hair.

A streak of light flashed across the sky, sending musical clacks into the air.

The Naculeans rejoiced.

And like an eagle with wings spread, the boys poised for a soaring flight. With Mark and Alina, they were embraced by the deep night, having been missed by the late evening's elements, and because they were needed in other places.

The five friends transformed into ambassadors for good, defenders of humanity, proud of their strengths and gifts.

Now passionate about their destiny, their focus came into view. With one step toward the hope of tomorrow, they sped into the night, leaving an elegant trail of awe and inspiration behind them.

And moment by moment the blades of grass enshrouded this secret, and their story became locked within, forever embedded in a mysterious place of wonder. And there, it would evolve under the watchful protection of the deepest elements of a midnight sky.

# Author
## *K.N. Smith*

K.N. Smith, winner of the "Best of" in the category of "Outstanding Young Adult Novel" at the Jessie Redmon Fauset Book Awards, is an author, screenwriter, and passionate advocate of literacy and arts programs throughout the world. She inspires people of all ages to reach their highest potential in their creative, educational, and life pursuits. She lives in California with her family. Visit K.N. Smith at www.knsmith.com.

# *Ordering Information*

To order from the author's website, please visit
www.knsmith.com

For orders by libraries and academic institutions, please
contact Baker & Taylor:

www.baker-taylor.com

For orders by U.S. trade bookstores and wholesalers,
please contact Ingram:

www.ingramcontent.com

For single print orders and Kindle or Nook e-books,
please visit:

www.amazon.com or www.bn.com

E-Books in other formats are available through all major
e-book retailers.

The saga continues...

# *The Energy of the Light*
Book #2 in **The Urban Boys** series

For details, visit www.knsmith.com

# THE
# URBANBOYS™
## DISCOVERY OF THE FIVE SENSES